BONE

BY

KEN FARMER

Cover Design by: Ken Farmer

THE AUTHOR

Ken Farmer didn't write his first full novel until he was sixty-nine years of age. He often wonders what the hell took him so long. At age seventy-six…he's currently working on novel number twenty-three---*Bone's Law*.

Ken spent thirty years raising cattle and quarter horses in Texas and forty-five years as a professional actor (after a stint in the Marine Corps). Those years gave him a background for storytelling…or as he has been known to say, "I've always been a bit of a bull---t artist, so writing novels kind of came naturally once it occurred to me I could put my stories down on paper."

Ken's writing style has been likened to a combination of Louis L'Amour and Terry C. Johnston with an occasional Hitchcockian twist…now that's a combination.

In addition to his love for writing fiction, he likes to teach acting, voice-over and writing workshops. His favorite expression is: "Just tell the damn story."

Writing has become Ken's second life: he has been a Marine, played collegiate football, been a Texas wildcatter, cattle and horse rancher, professional film and TV actor and now...a novelist. Who knew?

Web page: www.KenFarmer-Author.net

ACKNOWLEDGMENT

The author gratefully acknowledges T.C. Miller, Mary Deal, and Lt. Colonel Clyde DeLoach, USMC (Ret.) for their invaluable help in proofing and editing this novel.

ISBN-13: - 978-1-7329119-0-1 Paper
ISBN-10: - 1-7329119-0-8
Timber Creek Press
Imprint of Timber Creek Productions, LLC
312 N. Commerce St.
Gainesville, Texas 76240

Published by: Timber Creek Press
timbercreekpresss@yahoo.com
www.timbercreekpress.net
Twitter: @pagact
Facebook Book Page:
www.facebook.com/TimberCreekPress
Ken's email: pagact@yahoo.com
214-533-4964

DEDICATION

BONE is dedicated to my grand daughters, Makena and Morgan. I couldn't be more proud of anyone than I am of them. I also dedicate this novel to my brothers and sisters in the United States Marine Corps. Oorah! Semper Fi.

TIMBER CREEK PRESS

CHAPTER ONE

PARIS, TEXAS

"When the Assistant Secretary of the Navy reaches the Seven Devil Hills up in the Kiamichi Mountains on his hunting trip, that's when you and your men move, got it?...Kill his entourage, kidnap the Secretary and take him to the hideout."

"Hear tell he's purty salty an' good with a gun, Boss," said Brewster.

"What of it? You got enough men…Don't care if that four-eyed, blue nose is old scratch himself. You know the plan…just take care of it."

The boss opened a hand-carved walnut humidor, pulled out an expensive Cuban cigar, smelled the length of it, and then snipped the end off with his cutter. He picked up his new pistol-shaped silver lighter, warmed the cigar, lit it and blew a ring of blue aromatic smoke over his balding head.

The portly, well-dressed man removed the cigar from his mouth, held it up and rolled it through his fingers, looking at the burning end.

"Teddy Roosevelt is going to make us a lot of money," the boss said as his rough-dressed gunman, Tarlton Brewster, opened the paneled mahogany door and left.

A nondescript young man in a gray three-piece suit and black bowler sat on a bench across the street. He held an open newspaper in his hands as if he were reading it, but was actually looking just over the top at Brewster as he left the two story brick building.

BONE

The slender gunman untied his bay horse tethered to a ring in an iron post set in the concrete sidewalk, mounted and rode down the red brick street north toward the edge of town.

The man in the bowler glanced down the street at a large black cowboy leaning against a lamp post in front of the Red River Saloon, rolling a smoke and nodded.

The cowboy pitched the unlit quirly to the street as he untied his dapple gray stallion from a hitchrail, mounted, and followed Brewster out of town at a discrete distance.

The watcher in the suit folded the newspaper, stuck it under his arm, strolled down to the end of the block to the Western Union and Cable office and entered.

JACKSBORO, TEXAS
SHERIFF'S OFFICE

Sheriff Flynn put down the stub of a yellow #2 pencil he'd been writing on a tablet with. "Well, looks like the total reward on Wild Bob an' his gang comes to five thousand, five hundred

3

dollars…You and Loraine will have some money to live on…before you go find a way to go back to your time…assumin' that you do."

"Yeah, like we say in the Marine Corps…Improvise, adapt, and overcome…Is that on the first time or the second?" asked the giant of a man sitting on the corner of the sheriff's desk.

Flynn furrowed his brow and looked up. "Good question, Bone…does it matter?"

"Well, yeah. Need to share it with you and Fiona if it was the second."

"In my humble opinion, it would be the first, since they escaped while under my control."

"Still think we should share it with you…After all ya'll have another mouth to feed on the way." Loraine winked at Fiona.

"Now, sweet Loraine, we don't need it, but thank you for the consideration…We don't depend on our salaries as law enforcement officers to live off of…We've collected more than our share of rewards in the last few years…So there."

"I'd say let's go down to the bank an' I'll sign off on the disbursement of the bounties…You can open an account."

"Super! Then we can go to Barber's, buy some clothes, get some rooms at the hotel or that Polly's Boarding House and have a nice, long, hot bath," said Loraine. "Tired of trying to stay upwind from Bone."

"Need to take a whiff of yourself, Double D." He grinned, stuck up his massive hand and caught the cup the attractive, ample breasted, Hispanic woman threw at him.

"Damn you, Bone, one of these times you're going to miss."

"Not likely…Say, is there a laundry around we can send these things to?…Might need 'em." He poured some coffee in the cup and handed it back to Loraine.

"There's Sing Lu's just this side of Mom Tucker's Livery," said Fiona.

"Noticed it. Maybe they can sew up that hole." Loraine stuck her finger in the bullet hole in Bone's upper chest.

"Ow, that's still a bit tinder, Pard." He looked back at Mason. "What will the bank say about our social security numbers?" asked Bone.

"Your what?"

"Social…"

Loraine Rodriquez interrupted her partner. "Don't have social security until 1935, Bone."

"Oh, right, knew that...Probably a good thing."

"What's social security?" asked Fiona.

"It's a program instituted by the government that takes a percentage of what people make in their lifetime and then pay it back to them monthly when they reach age sixty-five. They call it the federal Old-Age, Survivors, and Disability Insurance program," replied Loraine.

"And the government administers it?" Fiona inquired.

"Uh, oh," commented Flynn.

"You got that right, Sheriff," said Bone nodding. "They can screw up an anvil."

"Well, not happenin' yet, so let's trundle down to the Cattlemen's Bank of Jacksboro an' take care of business...Shall we?"

"We're with you, Sheriff," replied Loraine. She took a last sip of her coffee and set the white porcelain mug on Mason's desk.

The others got up and headed out the door followed by the red and white Border Collie, Newton. Bone and Loraine were a few feet behind Mason and Fiona.

BONE

Loraine leaned toward Bone and whispered, "Are you not going to tell them you're their great grandson?"

"Still thinkin' on that. They got enough on their plate right now. Don't know that it'll serve any purpose...Maybe later."

She shook her head. "Your choice...They already know we're from the future."

He chuckled. "What would I call them...Grandma an' Grandpa?"

"Not unless you want to get shot," she replied with a grin.

"True."

Thirty minutes later, they walked out of the bank.

"Good thing you were with us, Mason. That banker was sure looking at us funny...Especially since it's a joint account an' we're not married," said Bone.

"I thought he was looking at us funny because of your signature," commented Loraine.

"What do you mean," asked Fiona. "I couldn't see it from where I was sitting."

"Instead of his name he drew an outline of a bone," answered Flynn.

"Really?" exclaimed Fiona.

Bone got a silly grin on his face. "When we go to the range to qualify twice a year, we get paper targets…After firing the requisite number of rounds at the required distances, we have to sign our targets and turn them in…Just got in the habit of drawing a bone…It stuck."

"Just be glad his first name is Darrell and not Peter," quipped Loraine.

"What?…Oh!" Fiona said and then blushed.

Bone shrugged his shoulders. "What can I say?"

Flynn chuckled. "Yeah…Well, least you got some walkin' around money, Bone," he said. "An' smart to use the address of Cletus an' Mary Lou's ranch, too."

"Good idea puttin' five grand in the bank and keepin' two fifty each. Now let's go get some clothes. Hate to give up my BDUs…"

"What are BDUs?" Fiona interrupted Bone.

He pointed at their camo cargo pants. "These…Stands for Battle Dress Utilities. Can carry a lot of stuff in these big pockets on the side…There's eight pockets altogether and the trousers are made out of a what they call a rip-stop material."

"I like the fact that they blend in with woods an' foliage," added Flynn.

"Like wearing buckskins on the trail. I've got a full set...including knee-high Apache style moccasins," said Fiona.

"Love to have some," commented Loraine. "And a pair of those knee-high moccasins you mentioned."

"I can sent ya'lls measurements to my grandmother up in the Nations just outside of Tahlequah...she's Cherokee. She and some of her friends can make you both a set in a week or so," offered Fiona.

"Cool," said Bone. "Got to thinkin'..."

"That's scary," quipped Loraine.

"Keep it up, Pard, just keep it up," Bone replied.

She got a big grin across her face. "Plan to."

"Got to thinkin' that mercantile may not have much in my size." He glanced at some of the people on the street there in Jacksboro.

"Got a point there, Detective Bone," said Flynn. "May have to go by a seamstress'. We got several in town. They can measure you and make whatever you want…Should be able to get jeans and a union suit, though…Need to get a hat, too."

"Damn, hate to lose my cap." He reset his department issue baseball type hat on his head.

"Makes you stick out like a sore thumb, Bone," said Loraine. "Not that you need a whole lot of help."

"Point," he replied.

Flynn opened the right side of the twin nine-foot tall half glass door for the others, ringing the two inch brass bell attached to the header. He followed them inside the fifty-foot wide mercantile.

"Huh, this is almost like a Walmart back home. Got everything from hardware, to guns an' ammo, to clothes and groceries," said Loraine.

"There's a better gun store down the street. They just carry guns and ammunition. The owner's a gunsmith, too," commented Fiona. "Can custom make a lot of stuff like holsters and specialty ammunition…He tuned up Mason's Peacemaker to be like mine."

"How's that?" asked Bone.

She took out her right hand .38-40 Colt, opened the gate and ejected the live rounds, closed it and spun the cylinder and held it up. "See how the hammer is flattened and flared to my thumb side?"

"Uh, huh," replied Loraine.

"It makes it much easier and a lot faster to just drag the side of my thumb across it to cock it as I draw. I can squeeze the trigger as soon as I clear the holster...Plus the trigger pull is a little less than two pounds."

"Holy cow...like a feather," exclaimed Bone. "May have him see what he can do for my 500...and see if he can make me some ammo along with a holster and gunbelt like ya'lls."

"Doubt he can do much for my Kimber 1911 Stainless Classic II...Got a seven round magazine plus one in the chamber."

"Double action, isn't it?" asked Fiona.

"Yes...Trigger pull is about 4.5 pounds. May see if he can soften that up a little...Kinda used to it, though," Loraine replied.

"Like to try it sometime."

"Me too," said Mason.

"Like to try your's too," Loraine said.

"We should go out behind the office later an' do some target practice," offered the sheriff.

"That'll work…Need to check on some .50 cal ammo first, though," said Bone.

"We'll go by Newly's Gun Shop after lunch."

"Sounds like fun," commented Loraine as she started going through some clothes Fiona had directed her to.

"The dresses are over against that wall," said Fiona as she pointed.

Loraine looked askance at the tall marshal. "Uh, I rarely find occasion to wear a dress, Fiona. Not much call for it in my line of work…unless I go undercover."

Fiona grinned. "My sentiments exactly."

Bone glanced over at the two very attractive women. "Ya'll make a pair, you know…Loraine's 5' 3" and you're what, Fiona, about 5' 11"?"

She grinned. "An even six feet in my stockings. Got my height from my Italian grandfather. He was about your height."

"You don't say? What a coincidence," said Bone with a smile.

"You and Loraine make quite a partnership too…6' 8" and 5' 3"," added Mason.

"Yeah, she hides under my arm like a duckling when it rains."

BONE

"Damn you, Bone, gonna kill you one of these days."

"You're too late, Pard, already been killed once," he countered, grinning.

"Well, it didn't take," she said as she picked up some black canvas riding pants with leather inserts in the seat and down the inside of the leg like the ones Fiona wore. "Have to have the legs trimmed off these some."

"Yeah, Loraine had to sue the city back home."

"Really? What for?" asked Fiona.

"She said they built the sidewalks too close to her butt."

"Damn you, Bone." Loraine looked around for something to throw…

§§§

CHAPTER TWO

BARBER'S MERCANTILE
JACKSBORO, TEXAS

"Hey, look here…How about this?" Bone held up a dark green John Bull hat and put it on. "Wow, fits too."

"Looks like the one Clint Eastwood wore in *Pale Rider*," said Loraine.

"Who?" asked Flynn.

"Clint Eastwood…he's a big movie star in our time," said Bone.

"Movie star?" asked Fiona. "Oh, like that moving picture thing Edison invented he called a Kinetograph back in 1890."

"Sort of that was the genesis of movies…In our time they make two to four hour full-length dramas with sound and in color…like plays, but with movin' pictures. You go in a dark theater and watch them projected on a big silver screen. They're fun…Cowboys and Indians, cops and robbers, war films, love stories, musicals…you name it," said Loraine.

"Right…Bat Masterson filmed a fight between Gentleman Jim Corbet and the Great John L. Sullivan last year in Garden City, Kansas…Got to watch the fight," commented Fiona.

"You worked with Bat Masterson?" asked Loraine.

"Sure. Bass Reeves, too…As you know, Bone," commented Fiona.

"Love to work with him. He's a real lawman, exclaimed Bone. "They will erect a larger than life-size bronze statue of him on his horse Flash in 2014 in front of the new US Marshals Service museum they're building in Fort Smith, Arkansas...The Marshals Service considers Bass to be the greatest marshal in their history." He glanced at Fiona. "Present company excepted, of course."

"Oh, goodness no. I'm not even in Bass Reeves' category. I felt like Jane in *McGuffey's First Eclectic Reader* when I worked with him...He's amazing."

"Don't let her kid you. She's been called the female Bass Reeves...and she doesn't backwater to any man," said Mason.

"Oh, you hush up," she replied.

A young man wearing a flat-topped Western Union and Cable cap entered, ringing the bell over the door again, and glanced around until he spotted Fiona. He approached and removed his hat. "Marshal Flynn?"

She turned. "Yes?"

He handed her a yellow envelope. "Telegram from Washington."

"Thank you." She opened it with her fingernail, extracted the flimsy and read it.

"Will there be an answer, Marshal?" the freckled-faced teenager asked, taking out a note pad and a stub of a yellow pencil.

She nodded. "Will comply...Stop...Leave for Paris on Thursday...Stop...Board train in Gainesville...Stop...Special Deputy US Marshal F.M. Flynn...End." She handed the messenger a Morgan silver dollar. "Keep the change, young man."

"Wow! Thank you, Ma'am."

"You're welcome...and don't ever call me, 'Ma'am'."

"Oh, yes...Uh, Marshal." He nodded to her, put his cap back on and headed quickly to the door.

When he had left, she looked first at her husband, and then turned to Bone and Loraine. She held up the telegram.

"From the Office of the United States Marshal through the US Secret Service...That's interesting...Looks like ya'll are going to get to meet the legendary Bass Reeves after all." She grinned big.

"Well, you're not goin', Missus Flynn."

Her steel-gray eyes snapped to her husband. "Oh, really? And pray tell why not, Mister Flynn?"

"You're pregnant."

"Oh, fiddlesticks, I'm barely two months along...I'll be the one to decide when I back off,

Mason Flynn." She gave him that look that would melt steel.

"See, that look? What'd I tell you?" he replied. "Here's Sewell's." Flynn held the door open. "After you."

"Thought you'd never ask," Bone said with a grin.

They headed over to Flynn's regular table against the far wall and took their chairs. The day waitress, Molly Sewell, Ruth Ann's sister, walked up, pad in hand.

"Sheriff, Miz Flynn, welcome." The attractive middle-aged brown-haired woman looked at Loraine and Bone. "Who are your friends?"

"Oh, sorry, Molly, you weren't here last night. This is Detective Darrell Bone an' Inspector Rodriquez...They're...uh, from out of town."

"Just call me Loraine, Molly," she said with a big grin.

"And just call me Bone...Heard a song about you, once."

Molly perked up and smiled. "Really?"

"Yeah, it was titled *Good Golly, Miss Molly*..."

"Don't sing it, Bone...especially not before we eat," said Loraine.

"You sayin' I can't sing, Pard?"

"Well, let's just say that pack of coyotes we heard tuning up the other night would accept you as part of the choir."

"Ouch."

Molly giggled. "What'll it be for ya'll, today?"

"What's the special?" asked Flynn.

"Ruth Ann's fried chicken or pan steak, smashed potatoes an' cream gravy, fried okra an' buttered squash with hot yeast rolls...Buttermilk pie for desert."

"Oh, yum...pan steak sounds good for me," answered Bone. "And love me some buttermilk pie."

"Me, too," said Fiona.

"Three," added Flynn

"And I'll take the chicken," commented Loraine.

"Guess we'd better gear up, check on that ammo at Newly's and see about Fiona taking our measurements for those buckskins," said Bone.

"I can have my Cherokee grandmother ship them to Paris from Tahlequah on the southbound train...It won't take her and her friends three or four days maximum to make them once I send her the measurements by telegram," commented Fiona.

"Are you part Cherokee, then, Fiona?" asked Loraine.

"No, not really. She's my first husband's grandmother. I just stayed close to her after he died."

"Oh, I'm sorry to hear. Was he ill?" inquired Loraine.

Fiona shook her head. "He was murdered...right in front of my eyes in our mercantile store in Tahlequah by a renegade Cherokee...That's the reason I learned to shoot and became a Deputy US Marshal under Judge Parker in Fort Smith."

"The hangin' Judge," commented Bone.

"That's right. I eventually was assigned to Bass Reeves and tracked down the renegade, Calvin Mankiller..."

"Appropriate name," said Loraine.

"Yes, it was. Tried to arrest him but he wasn't having any of it and I shot him twice in the chest. He fell into the Red River...We couldn't find the body."

"Don't tell me he didn't die an' came back?"

"That's right..."

Bone interrupted her. "I thought you weren't going to tell me."

Fiona shook her head and took a breath. "He went on a killing and burning spree and Brushy Bill Roberts and I...

"Brushy Bill? Isn't he the guy that said he was really Billy the Kid?" asked Bone.

Fiona glanced around the restaurant and started to speak when Molly came back carrying two of their orders.

"Loraine, here's yours and Fiona's...Be right back boys." She headed back to the kitchen.

"He is Billy the Kid...He and his friend, Sheriff Pat Garrett, faked his death. He disappeared down in Mexico for a couple of years, and then came back as Brushy Bill Roberts." Fiona stopped and smiled.

"Bill became a horse thief detective for the railroad...then a Pinkerton detective and now a Special US Deputy Marshal, like me, out of Washington...You'll get to meet him, I'm sure," said Fiona.

"Holy cow. Goin' to meet Bass Reeves an' Billy the Kid...Who knew?" said Bone.

"And probably Bodie Hickman, too," added Mason.

"Texas Ranger Bodie Hickman?" exclaimed Loraine.

Fiona nodded. "Brushy Bill and Bodie both headquarter in Gainesville."

Bone and Loraine exchanged glances.

§§§

CHAPTER THREE

NEWLY'S GUN SHOP
JACKSBORO, TEXAS

They entered the small gun shop that was permeated with the wonderful smell of gun oil and leather.

A slight-built man with a full mustache, wearing a leather apron, looked up from his work table behind a glass counter with two full shelves of different types of handguns on display. Some of the guns were new and some were used.

"Hey, Newly," greeted Mason.

He put down a leather working tool and a small wooden mallet, got to his feet and walked around the counter. "Sheriff Flynn…Marshal Flynn, glad to see ya'll." He stuck out his hand.

Mason shook it. "Let me introduce you to some friends of ours from out of town…This is Darrell Bone and Loraine Rodriquez. They're law officers from…uh, back east."

"Just call me, Bone."

"And me, Loraine…It's a pleasure."

"How can I help ya'll," asked Newly.

Bone pulled his .50 cal from its holster clipped to his web belt, opened the cylinder and dumped out the five rounds in his hand. "Can you make me any of these?" He handed him one of the brass shells.

"Wow, .50 cal. What kind of weapon is that?…Never seen anything like it."

"Smith & Wesson 500…It's an…uh, experimental model," stammered Bone. "I like a 350 or 400 grain bullet an' these have the…uh, new smokeless powder."

"May I?" Newly held out his hand for the gun. "Oh, my." He grinned from ear to ear as he hefted it and felt the balance. "A real hand cannon."

Bone nodded. "It is that…Can you help me?"

"I can cast the bullets easy enough, even with this flat nose." He looked up at the big man. "And I just got in a twenty pound can of that smokeless powder you mentioned. They've been using it in the military for about eight years an' just released it to public dealers like me."

"So you can duplicate these rounds for me, then?"

"I can. How many do you need?"

"Oh…" He looked at Fiona. "…Couple hundred rounds?"

She nodded.

"How about some of these in the smokeless?" asked Loraine as she pulled her Kimber, ejected the magazine and pushed out one of the .45 caliber rounds.

"My goodness, another weapon I've never seen."

"It's also an experimental, but, it's a semiautomatic…uh, from Germany," said Loraine.

"Read about those. May I keep them overnight? Want to make sure the rounds fit for each weapon…"

Bone and Loraine exchanged glances.

"By the way," said Bone. "Also need a holster like the Sheriff's…with loops for at least twenty to thirty rounds on the belt."

"Same for me, except I have three of these magazines I need to carry on the belt…with loops for as many refills of loose rounds that will fit." Loraine held up her seven round mag.

"Can do that, too." He got out a cloth measuring tape. "Let me measure where you're goin' to wear it."

"Hope you have enough strap leather for her belt…Expect she's going to wear it around her hips," commented Bone.

"Damn you, Bone." Loraine turned to Newly. "Let me have my gun back. I'm going to shoot this big galoot."

"Don't do it." Bone held up his hands to the gunsmith and grinned.

Newly chuckled at their antics. "When do ya'll need all this?"

"What time is it? asked Bone.

He chuckled again and nodded. "Have everything ready by ten in the mornin'…Promise," he commented. "I've got to shoot these…Test the rounds, you know."

He wrapped the tape around Bone, just below the top of his pants and jotted the measurement down. "Now you, Loraine. Point the spot."

She placed her finger tips on both sides just above her hip bones. "Here."

"See?" said Bone. Then he turned to Flynn and grinned. "Like a kid in a candy store."

"Absolutely," said Newly smiling. "How many rounds do you need, Loraine?"

"Three hundred?"

"I can do that. I work late most nights anyway…Not work when you love what you do."

"We'll be over at Polly's Boarding House, if you need us," said Bone. "And you can see if you can soften up the trigger spring like you did Mason's .45…if you would."

"And mine, too. It's about 4.5 pounds now," added Loraine.

"Oh, need a cleaning kit for the .50…You too, Pard?"

She nodded.

"I can fix somethin' up, I'm sure," replied Newly. "My hired help and apprentice…high school boy named Harley Ford…will be here 'bout two o'clock. He can help me do the rounds."

"Much obliged, Newly," said Bone.

"Let's have a beer at the Coolwater Saloon before ya'll check in at Polly's," suggested Flynn.

"Hey, sounds like a deal to me," said Bone. "Lead the way."

They walked down the block a short way, crossed the dirt street and stepped over or around the scattered piles of horse apples.

"If ya'll need anything else, I'm sure you can get it at Buck Stienke's Lone Star Shooting Supply in Gainesville," said Fiona. "We're going to spend the night there, anyway."

"Good to know," replied Bone.

Stepping up on the boardwalk, they pushed through the bat wing doors of the saloon.

Flynn and Fiona habitually moved to the right to get out of the back glare from outside.

"Wow, just like in the movies," Bone leaned over and whispered to Loraine, as they too moved over.

BONE

"Never realized from the movies that they smelled like stale beer, tobacco smoke, vomit and urine," she commented.

"Just like the honky-tonks back home."

"Point." Loraine nodded.

After their eyes adjusted to the dim light, they sauntered to the thirty-five foot long polished walnut bar that ran along the right side of the room.

The slim, middle-aged, balding bartender walked up from behind the bar. A white bar towel was slung over his shoulder.

"What'll it be, Sheriff?" he asked.

Flynn looked at the others. "Cold Lone Star for me, Truman...Ya'll?"

"Wow, you got Lone Star?" asked Bone.

"Just ordered it, didn't I," responded Flynn.

"Sounds good," said both Fiona and Loraine.

"Cool...Just barely run mine over," said Bone.

Truman looked up at the big man and grinned. "I'll bring a wash tub."

"Man after my own heart," Bone commented as Truman turned and walked toward the beer spigots.

The bartender returned with four large mugs. Each had a full head of foam.

"To a new venture with the legendary Bass Reeves," said Bone as he held up his mug.

"I assure you that he doesn't think of himself as legendary," commented Fiona with a smile. "He's a very humble man...But, I've never seen him exhibit the slightest indication of fear...under any circumstances."

Three cowboys burst through the doors and headed to the bar. They hadn't waited for their eyes to adjust and the smallish man in the lead bumped into Bone's back, causing him to spill beer on the front of his shirt.

He turned and looked down at the cowboy who was at least a foot shorter than he was. "Need to watch where you're goin', there, little man."

"Little man, my ass...Why is it all you big bastards got to think you can lord over everbody." The small man took a wild haymaker swing.

Bone caught his fist in midair and held it for a moment before he let it go. "Now, pal, why don't you an' your friends move on down the bar an' have your drinks...First one's on me...What say?"

"The hell with you," said the already inebriated cowboy from a previous stop. "I'm fixin' to stomp a mud hole in your big ass deep enough to bury a wagon in."

Bone grinned. "Not likely."

"Oh, yeah?"

The little cowboy stepped up and started wind milling with both fists. Bone just put his hand in the man's face and held him at arm's length.

The cowboy finally backed up, grabbed a bow chair and started to swing it.

Bone raised his ham-like right hand into a hammer fist and brought it down sharply on top of the little man's head, crushing the crown of his hat and dropping him to the sawdust covered floor like a pile of wet string.

"Always happens that way. Little guys with a Napoleon complex gotta walk around with a chip on their shoulder," said Bone as he took a long swig of what was left of his beer.

Truman handed him a fresh mug and a clean bar towel to wipe his T-shirt down while he cleaned up the spilled beer from the bar.

The little cowboy staggered to his feet, blinking and rubbing the back of his neck, and then pushing his hat back up off his ears. "What the hell did you hit me with, big man?"

Bone grinned and glanced over his shoulder at him. "A sample."

"Now I'd suggest you do like he said. You an' your friends move on down the bar an' have your drinks," said Flynn.

"An' like I said..." Bone looked at Truman. "...on me."

The little man nodded with new respect to Bone and replied to Mason. "Right, Sheriff...Yessir, right away."

The three moved off and took places down the bar.

When they were out of earshot, Bone turned to Fiona and whispered. "Any idea what this little trip to Paris is about?"

She glanced around to make sure there was no one else listening. "No idea, Bone. They never explain the purpose in a telegram..."

"Can understand that," interrupted Loraine.

"...but, with the Secret Service involved, that tells me it has something to do with either counterfeiting or the administration...or both."

"Oh, that's right. It was originally formed to check the rampant flood of counterfeit currency an' assist the Office of the United States Marshal with murders, bank robberies and illegal gambling about the time the war ended," commented Bone.

Fiona nodded. "Correct…and still does."

"I was surprised to learn the Secret Service was formed by Allan Pinkerton," added Bone.

"Really?" exclaimed Loraine.

"Yep, he was an undercover spy for the Union in the War of Northern Aggression, as we refer to it in Texas," added Bone.

"I didn't know that," commented Flynn.

Bone grinned and nodded. "Now you do."

"Is there gonna be a quiz?"

"I'll think on it," replied Bone.

"I suspect we'll find out what this is all about in short order when we meet up with Bass…I would surmise it's fairly serious. They don't send him on minor crimes," commented Fiona.

"And just so ya'll know, to Bass Reeves, the law isn't everything…It's the only thing," added Fiona.

"Wouldn't expect anything less from him," added Bone.

"Did the telegram say where we'll find him," asked Loraine.

Fiona shook her head and smiled. "Won't be necessary…He'll find us when we get to Paris…Trust me."

"Why is that not a surprise," said Bone.

§§§

CHAPTER FOUR

POLLY'S BOARDING HOUSE
JACKSBORO, TEXAS

Fiona rolled up the measuring tape she had borrowed from Polly downstairs. She wrote the final measurements on a slip of paper.

"Well, that should do it...Husband, why don't you and I sash-shay down to the telegraph office and send this off to my grandmother...I'm sure

Loraine and Bone want to get settled in, have those hot baths and put on some clean clothes."

"Well, you can sash-shay, my love...think I'll mosey," commented Flynn as he swatted her on her shapely bottom.

"You can do that a little slower...if you wish," she said with a twinkle in her eye.

Flynn matched the gleam. "Later."

Loraine grinned at them. "So looking forward to that bath and clean clothes."

"Actually, I am too. Can't hardly stand my ownself," added Bone.

"I can believe that," commented Loraine. "If you'll step across the hall to your room, Bone, I've got first dibs on the bath down at the end of the hall...Polly said she'd have the tub ready."

"Don't want to share, huh?" he asked.

"Only in your dreams, Bone...Only in your dreams...and if you try to use that bracelet Lucy gave you and become invisible, swear to God I'll shoot you right between the eyes when you turn it back on."

"Don't have your Kimber, remember?...Left it with Newly."

She reached in her saddlebags on the bed and pulled out the .44-40 Remington Flynn had given her. "What's this…smart aleck?"

"Oh…yeah…Forgot about that."

"Don't understand why you two aren't married," said Fiona, shaking her head.

"Not if he was the last man on earth…"

"Or woman," Bone interrupted Loraine. "We have been married a couple of times…"

"For undercover work," Loraine quickly interrupted him.

"Had to track down a serial killer…but we like to have killed one another before we got him," said Bone.

Flynn shook his head and grabbed Fiona's elbow. "See ya'll about six an' we'll head to supper…Let's go my dear, by the time we get back, maybe they'll either have finished their toi-letties or shot each other an' then we can take *our* baths…Together?" He flicked his eyebrows up and down twice.

"Could be, Mason Flynn…Could be," Fiona replied with a devilish gleam in her steel-gray eyes as they walked out into the hallway and headed downstairs.

Bone stepped across the hall to his room a moment later. "Knock on my door when you're done. We'll take our stuff down to Sing Lu's after I wash off the big chunks."

"Hope he doesn't scream in fright," answered Loraine.

"Doubt it…You get a whiff of those cowboys that came in the saloon? They gotta have their clothes washed some time…Doesn't rain often enough around here to get rinsed off."

"You broke the first rule of law enforcement."

Bone frowned. "How so?"

"Making assumptions in the absence of facts."

"Ah…Got a point there, Pard…Maybe they wear 'em until they can stand up in the corner by themselves an' then just get new ones."

"Probably cheaper that way."

"Yep," he answered as he closed the door behind him.

Two hours later, Mason and Fiona knocked on Bone and Loraine's doors.

Bone stepped out in the hallway in blue bib farmer overalls, a long sleeved red union top and his dark green John Bull hat. The .45 Colt Peacemaker Flynn gave him was shoved in one of the deep back pockets.

Loraine had already joined the Flynns in her black morning coat, gray gabardine low cut vest over a white blouse and black canvas riding pants with the leather seat and inner thigh insert.

The three looked the big man up and down, all got big grins.

"Well, wouldn't say that's blending in, but don't see you got much choice," said the sheriff as he led the way down the hall to the stairs.

"Uh, huh, since that was the only stuff Mister Barber had that would fit him," added Fiona. "We can look in Gainesville or just may have to wait till my grandmother and her friends send the buckskins."

Loraine quipped. "Trust me, he doesn't care, one way or the other...The chief of police back home said Bone was the only person he ever met that honestly and truly just didn't give a damn."

Bone had bundled up their soiled modern clothes and had them under his arm. "Yep, he's pretty close, I'd say...Do care if my beer's cold or not, though...Let's boogie down to that Chinese fellow's place so we can drop this smelly stuff off an' then go grab a steak or pizza."

"What's 'boogie' and what's 'pizza'?" asked Flynn.

"Boogie is a fast-paced, rhythmic type of dancin' music back home and 'pizza' is one of the four food groups…and a staple," commented Bone.

"It's called pizza pie in Italy according to my grandfather. It's a large, round, flat bread crust covered with tomato sauce, mozzarella cheese, sausage, spices and other toppings and baked in an open brick oven," added Fiona. "The only places you can find pizza pie in America is New York, Chicago, Philadelphia, and wherever there are concentrations of Italian immigrants."

"So you're sayin' there's not a pizzeria in Jacksboro?" asked Bone.

"In a word…no, or in Gainesville, for that matter," Fiona answered. "And I doubt in Fort Worth, either."

Bone glanced at Loraine. "Well, know what kind of side business we can open up, Pard, if we're going to be stuck here a while…A pizzeria. Make a fortune."

"You might have a point there, Bone," said Fiona. "I do love a good Italian sausage pizza pie."

"Me too…Every once in a while Bone can come up with a good idea.

They reached Sing Lu's Laundry and went in the front door.

"Sheriff Frynn," said the diminutive Manchurian Chinese immigrant with a long black, streaked with gray, queue or pig tail hanging out from under his skull cap.

"Sing Lu…Brought you some customers."

"Velly good, Sheriff. Velly good. Sing Ru take good care." He pointed at the bundle under Bone's arm. "You give, prease. Sing Ru fix velly quick. Yes?"

Bone placed the dirty clothes on the counter that was between the front door and a curtain that closed off the Chinese women working over steaming wash pots in the back.

Sing Lu picked up a once white sock from the bundle and wrinkled his nose. "Uhh, may have radies wash two time…maybe tree. We get clean…You betcha."

He looked at the hole in Bone's T shirt on top of the pile. "Sing Ru, fix tear in shirt. Be rike new.

Sing Ru iron good, too...You come back in morning. We finish. Velly good."

Loraine gave Sing Lu a big smile and bowed slightly with her palms together. "*Xièxiè ni, gudài.*"

"You know Chinese customs?" asked Sing Lu.

Loraine nodded. "This unworthy one has earned a seventh level black belt in *Kung Fu* and *Wushu.*"

Sing Lu bowed back in the same manner. "For you, Sing Lu take extra care."

"*Xièxie,*" she replied and then turned to Flynn. "Shall we go?"

He nodded with a rather blank look on his face as he opened the door for the ladies to exit first.

"What was that you said in there, Pard?" asked Bone after they stepped out on the boardwalk.

She grinned. "Just said, 'thank you, ancient one' in Mandarin."

"Right." He looked back at her. "You got a seventh degree black belt in *Kung Fu*?...Knew you practiced it, but didn't know about the belts...Wow! Congrats, Pard...I'm impressed."

"And *Wushu*...It's kind of similar."

"What's *Kung Fu*?" asked Flynn.

"It's a form of Chinese martial arts and it means she can kick your butt any day of the week," said Fiona. "Without breaking a sweat."

"And twice on Sunday," added Bone.

"Ever had to use it in your work?" asked Flynn.

Loraine blushed slightly. "On occasion…Handy for disarming and subduing a knife wielding assailant, a drunk…or a someone holding a gun on you within the strike zone."

"She can do it too," said Bone as he opened the door to Sewell's.

"Come in folks," greeted Molly.

She stepped aside, let them head to Flynn's regular table against the far wall and followed them over with her note pad.

Flynn started to speak, but was interrupted by Bone.

"Just a second, Sheriff, got an idea."

"Uh, oh," muttered Loraine.

"Molly, you reckon Fiona and me can go back in the kitchen an' show Ruth Ann a new dish?"

"New dish?"

"Yeah, it's called a pizza pie," he said.

"If it's a pie, Ruth Ann can make it," Molly commented.

"Bet she can too."

Bone got to his feet and pulled Fiona's chair out and they followed Molly to the kitchen.

"This should be interestin'," said Flynn.

"One thing about Bone…He borders on what can be called a gourmet cook," commented Loraine.

"Had no idea."

"Don't tell him I said so."

Twenty minutes later, Bone and Fiona returned, each with big grins.

"Ya'll are goin' to be blown away in about fifteen minutes," said Bone. "We were lucky Ruth Ann already had a big bowl of yeast dough under a towel…Didn't take but a minute to show her how to make a large flat bread crust to put the ingredients on."

"We laid out all the toppings and cheese and whipped up some marinara tomato sauce for her…She didn't have any Italian sausage, so we used some venison and pork sausage, spices, onion, bell peppers and mushrooms…With a little grated brick cheese sprinkled on top of the mozzarella."

"No pepperoni I suppose?" asked Loraine.

"Didn't have pepperoni till 1919," replied Bone.

"Oh, didn't know," she responded.

"Bone went out back, found a wide piece of cedar shingle to use as a spatula to put the pie in the oven and to take it out when it was ready." Fiona grinned and glanced at Bone. "Won't be long now."

Molly stepped back over to the table. "Ruth Ann is like a kid with a new toy. She's makin' an extra one for her and me...What can I get ya'll to drink?"

"Well, since you don't have beer, guess I'll have iced tea," said Bone.

"Works for me," commented Flynn.

"Make it four," added Loraine. "With a sprig of mint in mine."

"Mine, too," said Fiona.

By the time Molly came back with a tray carrying the tea, Ruth Ann was behind her with a large platter normally saved for serving Thanksgiving turkey, but now had the steaming, fragrant, pizza pie covering the entire surface.

She had a large butcher knife in her dress side pocket she pulled out and handed to Bone. "I'm sure you'd like the honors, Mister Bone," Ruth Ann said with a grin.

"Thank you, Madam…and it's just plain Bone." He took the large knife, placed the edge in the middle, rocked it back and forth and then moved it over and across the pie repeatedly until he had cut it into eight pie-shaped wedges.

He slipped the broad knife under a slice, lifted it up and laid it in Loraine's plate. He did the same for Fiona, Mason, and finally his own.

"All right folks…This is how you eat a pizza pie."

Bone picked up his slice, folded it lengthwise and stuck the narrow end in his mouth and took a big bite. A string of the melted cheese strung out as he pulled the wedge back. He rolled the folded wedge over until all the mozzarella was wrapped around the slice.

"That's how you do it…Oh, yum, that's good," Bone said as he closed his eyes and chewed with orgasmic pleasure.

The others quickly followed suit.

"Oh, my gosh," commented Flynn. "I have died and gone to heaven." He took another bite.

"You outdid yourself, Bone," said Loraine between bites.

He grinned. "I know."

The other patrons began to take notice of the delicious aroma of the Italian dish that had filled the restaurant and several motioned to Molly about what it was and to give her an order.

"Hope Ruth Ann has enough dough made up," commented Bone as he folded his second slice, and then took a big bite.

The door to the restaurant burst open and the barber from next door, Enos Glenn, ran in, straight to their table. "Sheriff, Sheriff, some men are robbin' the mercantile."

§§§

CHAPTER FIVE

SEWELL'S RESTAURANT
JACKSBORO, TEXAS

"How do you know, Enos?" asked Flynn as he wiped the marinara sauce from his chin.

"It's after six an' I seen five men ride up an' tie off in the front. Four of 'em forced their way inside while Mervin was tryin' to lock the door. One feller stayed outside, watchin' the horses...He kept lookin' around…all nervous like. Don't look good to me…no, sirree, Sheriff, shore don't," an excited Enos said.

The four law officers got to their feet as one and headed to the door.

Sheriff Flynn turned to the other customers in the restaurant. "Everbody stay inside, hear? And wouldn't hurt for ya'll to get down on the floor. Might be some shootin' goin' on out there…Don't want nobody catchin' a stray bullet."

Bone looked through the glass at the man with the horses across the street, and then eased the door open. He hand signaled Flynn and Fiona to the left and he and Loraine slipped out to the right.

"Get behind that water trough, Pard," he said softly.

"Where are you going?"

Bone got his patented grin across his face. "Believe I'll saunter across the street…That horse holder will think I'm just a local farmer come to town."

"You're nuts, Bone," Loraine whispered.

"So, what else is new?" He stepped out in the street and walked in the general direction of the Coolwater Saloon just to the left of the mercantile.

He whistled *Oh! Susanna*, with his hands in his pockets, as he walked.

The nervous outlaw with the horses only gave Bone a casual glance before looking back at the front door of Barber's.

"What the Sam Hill's he doin'?" Flynn whispered to Fiona from behind a stack of bagged oats in front of Smith's Feed store.

"Looks like to me he's using his new clothes as undercover...Pretty smart," she replied as she scrunched down behind a barrel of hoes, shovels and rakes a few feet away at the edge of the boardwalk.

"Damn, let's hope so." Flynn eased his .45 from his holster and thumbed a sixth round in the cylinder.

Bone altered his path slightly and stepped up on the boardwalk and turned to the outlaw on the horse next to the four others. "Say, pard, you got'ny fixin's? I done run out...Dyin' fer a smoke."

The man glanced at Bone then looked up and down the street and back to what he assumed was a local farmer. "Uh...shore." He pulled out a bag of Bull Durham from his vest pocket and pitched it to Bone.

"Uh...Keep it...Got another." He looked back at the front door of Barber's.

"Well, hey, much obliged." Bone stepped up on the boardwalk, took out a paper and shook some of the tobacco down the center.

The horse holder looked back down. "Nice hat."

"Thanks, found it." Bone pulled the string on the bag with his teeth, closing it, licked the edge of the paper, rolled it up and twisted the ends. "Got a match?"

"Well, damn," the man mumbled. "No! Go find somebody else..."

The right side of the double glass paneled doors of the mercantile burst open and four men rushed out, each had a couple of full cloth bags in their hands.

"Far enough, boys...Hands in the air. Fun's over for today," Bone said as he threw the unlit quirley to the street and whipped out the .45 from his back pocket and thumbed the hammer to full cock.

"Damn you," cried the horse holder as he drew his Colt and snapped a quick shot at Bone. The hurried round missed the big man and shattered one of the windows of Barber's.

He then wheeled his horse around and viciously dug his big roweled spurs in his mount's ribs and lashed his split reins over and under as the animal sprinted down the street toward the edge of town, kicking up dust and throwing small pebbles in his wake.

Bone dived to the street, losing his hat in the process. He rolled over and fired two rounds at the panicked robbers on the boardwalk.

They dropped the bags of merchandise and money they carried, drew their weapons while vainly trying to catch their frightened horses.

The outlaws turned and started firing at Fiona headed their way from across the street.

Flynn raised up from behind the stacked feed bags and cranked a shot at the man galloping by. The bullet plowed a furrow across the outlaw's back as he leaned forward just as the sheriff fired.

The other panicked horses galloped between Flynn and the escaping outlaw, foiling any additional shot he might have taken.

Down the boardwalk from Mason and Fiona, in front of the barber shop, Loraine raised up from behind the wooden water trough and fired at one of the robbers as he was trying to steal a horse tied in front of the saloon. Her shot caught him in the side and he dropped to the dusty street, writhing in pain.

Fiona, with a Colt in each hand, had stepped out from behind the implement barrel and deliberately walked across the street directly at the remaining two outlaws who were shooting at her. She was firing her .38-40 Peacemakers simultaneously as she coolly strode toward the robbers. Dirt kicked up around her feet from their ill-aimed bullets.

They didn't have a chance. Not only did each of her shots hit their marks, but, Bone's two rounds did also.

The outlaws jerked like marionettes on strings as each bullet impacted their bodies in rapid succession—then they both staggered back and collapsed on the boardwalk like so much dirty laundry.

The silence was deafening as the huge clouds of acrid white gunsmoke slowly drifted to the east down the street on the soft evening breeze.

Wide-eyed townsfolk peeked out from doors and alleyways where they had taken refuge when the first shots were fired.

Fiona glanced at Bone getting slowly to his feet across the street. "Are you hit, Bone?"

"Nope, just trying not to put my hand in a pile of horse turds," he replied as he put his hat back on. "But, what in hell did you think you were doin'?"

She grinned. "They were panic shooting. Almost impossible to hit anything that way."

"You just said 'almost'," he responded. "You reminded me of me."

Flynn, Loraine and Fiona gathered around Bone as he stepped over to the downed, would-be robbers.

"Damn, I'm used to them droppin' like shot doves when I hit 'em with the .50 cal…Took my two and Fiona's four bullets to knock these hoodlums to the ground," said Bone.

"The one I shot is still breathing," commented Loraine as she walked over to the moaning man in the street.

"Here comes Doc Mosier with his bag. Mind he figured he'd be needed when he heard the shootin'," added Flynn.

He turned and noticed the owner of the tonsorial parlor standing behind him. "Wanna go in an' check on Mervin, Enos? Didn't hear no shots from inside."

"Yessir," the proprietor of the tonsorial parlor said as he opened the door and rushed inside.

"Any of 'em alive?" the white-haired physician asked as he hurriedly walked up, out of breath.

"One," said Fiona pointing at the outlaw rolled up in a fetal position on the ground on the other side of a water trough.

He knelt down beside the wounded man, examined the entry wound and the exit wound, and then shook his head. "He's a goner...Liver shot." Mosier looked up at Loraine.

She nodded. "Thought so, when I saw how dark the blood was...Seen it before."

"Maybe I can give him some Laud..." He stopped and looked back down as the man breathed out a soft death rattle and his left heel drummed against the dusty street. "Well, no need."

Enos led a staggering fifty-year old owner of the mercantile from inside. Blood was trickling down the side of his face from a gash just inside the hairline. He was holding a new towel against the wound.

"Doc, one of them yahoos whacked Mervin upside the head with his gun barrel...Got a towel for him to hold on it for the bleedin'…He ain't none too steady."

"I noticed," said Mosier. "Sit him on that bench against the wall there, before he falls down."

Enos assisted Mervin to one of the green painted slat benches along the wall outside his store. "Here, have a sit, Merv," he said as Doctor Mosier lifted the folded towel to take a look at the wound, put it back, and then looked at the man's eyes.

He turned to several of the townspeople gathered around. "Some of you boys help Mervin to my office. He's going to need some stitches…Plus he's got a slight concussion…Be particular with him now."

Flynn looked down the street as the dust from the escaping outlaw settled to the ground. "Well, looks like ya'll are gonna have to go to Paris without me…Got a miscreant to track."

"Maybe we can delay the trip a few days and go with you," commented Bone.

"Naw, ain't but one…'Sides, purty sure I clipped him across the back when he rode by. Saw his coat tug…He ain't gonna be makin' very good time, is my guess…Ya'll go ahead. Bass'll be expectin' you." Flynn glanced over at Bone. "'Sides, you can keep an eye on my bride…"

"Mason Flynn, you know better than that. I was tracking and collaring outlaws on the scout long before we met, you know." She turned to Bone and Loraine. "While I appreciate the company and all, I'm quite capable of taking care of myself."

Bone grinned. "That's good to know, Fiona…sure wasn't looking forward to any more holes in me."

Loraine backhanded him across the chest. "Damn you, Bone, that was rude."

"It's all right, Loraine. He does have a point. I wouldn't be here if it weren't for Bone." She stepped over to him, hugged his neck and kissed his cheek. "I really haven't had a chance to say, 'Thank you.'"

"Well, I'll be…That's the first time I've ever seen him blush," said Loraine.

Bone snatched his John Bull hat from his head. "It's all right…Not used to being thanked for doin' my job."

"Saving my life is your job?…Why is that?" asked Fiona.

"I'll fill you in on that some other time…Fiona." He hugged her back.

She glanced over at Loraine. "I suppose you know, don't you?"

Loraine gave her a wry smile. "Know what?"

"That's what I thought."

"Well, if ya'll are through scratching each other's back. I'd say lets go finish our pizza and have some of Ruth Ann's buttermilk pie."

"Best idea I've heard today…Nothin' wrong with cold pizza anyway," commented Bone. "When are you taking out after that would-be robber?"

"In the mornin'. Like I said, don't think he's goin' to cover no whole lot of ground. Hard as hell to ride with a sore back…Gets much out of a walk, I'll be surprised."

"You just have to watch out for an ambush, my love," said Fiona.

He grinned at her. "Yes, Dear."

§§§

CHAPTER SIX

JACKSBORO, TEXAS
MOM TUCKER'S LIVERY

"Not goin' to take your pack horse, Potawatomi?" asked Mom Tucker as she removed her corncob pipe from her overalls chest pocket and packed it from a leather pouch.

"Slow me down, Mom. Takin' enough in my saddlebags for three or four days," Flynn replied.

"Sure you don't want one of us to go along?" asked Bone.

Flynn grinned as he buckled his bulging saddlebags behind his cantle, and then strapped on his soogan. "I think not. Ain't my first tail chase, Bone...I'll join up with ya'll after I take care of this yahoo."

"What about the office?" asked Loraine.

"Sent Bert out to get Slim Parker at Lisanne's after breakfast. He can take care of the ne'er-do-wells 'round here till I get back...The town marshal is purtnigh useless, but he does show a presence."

"Slim's a Chickasaw Freedman, isn't he?" inquired Bone.

Flynn nodded as he made a final check of the girth on his blue roan Morgan gelding, Laddie. "He was a regular deputy till he got a job of work helpin' Lisanne at her horse ranch."

"When's Doctor Mosier supposed to give the green light to Gomer?" asked Loraine.

"Green light?" asked Flynn.

"It's an expression from our time meaning..."

Bone interrupted her. "He's good to go."

"Oh...The doc said 'bout two weeks till his broke ribs heal up enough to get around without major pain."

"There's no telling how long our little foray over to Paris with Bass will take, either," said Fiona.

"You can probably recruit Bodie if the Rangers don't have him on a case," suggested Flynn.

"That would be way cool," commented Bone. "He's a real legend in Gainesville...in our time."

"Bodie Hickman?" asked Fiona.

"Uh, huh...Busted up a major oil theft crime ring up near Wichita Falls and a big time bank robbery over in Cisco in 1927," said Loraine.

Fiona and Mason exchanged glances and grins.

"I'll be dipped," commented Flynn. "Our Bodie...Who knew?"

"We'll be staying at the same place in Gainesville, Skeans Boarding House...He and Annabel and their twins live there...As does Brushy Bill," Fiona added.

"Bodie loves to work with Bass...His godfather, Deputy US Marshal Jack McGann, was Bass' partner for twenty-one years until they transferred Bass to the Paris office after Judge Parker passed away."

"How come they transferred Bass to Paris?" asked Bone.

"The new judge transferred or otherwise got rid of all the colored and Indian marshals workin' the territory within a month of taking over," said Flynn.

"Yeah, we still got a few of those racist types left in our time…less and less all the time, though, thank God," commented Loraine.

"Like Bass used to say about being a marshal in the Nations under Parker, 'The Judge don't care what color a man's skin is…it's how he does the job that counts'," said Fiona.

"He's never failed to serve a warrant since he became a marshal back in '75…I understand he's getting close to three thousand felony arrests…and Bass can't read or write."

"Can't read? How does he serve a warrant?" asked Bone.

"He has Jack or somebody read them to him as he looks at each one. Bass says that the names are like pictures to him and are as distinct as a horseshoe print when he's tracking…Once he sees it, he doesn't forget it…and he's never made a mistake."

"Wow, that's amazing," said Loraine.

"It's called having a photographic memory in our time," added Bone.

"That makes sense…Ya'll are going to love working with him," commented Fiona.

Flynn stabbed a foot in Laddie's stirrup and swung his leg easily over the six-inch cantle. "Enough of the history lesson, I gotta get on the trail while the gettin's good."

Newton spun around in a circle and woofed his pleasure at leaving.

Flynn leaned down and gave Fiona a long lingering kiss.

"You better cut that out, mister, if you still plan to leave…We can catch up when you join us in Paris." She pecked him affectionately on the lips again. "Take care…I love you."

"Love you, too, darlin'." He wheeled his mount about and with a wave over his shoulder to Bone and Loraine, nudged Laddie into an amble trot—a smooth four beat medium gait he could maintain for long periods, that can average eight to ten miles an hour. Newton trotted alongside.

They watched Flynn and the red and white border collie as he reined Laddie north at the edge of town.

"Tracks must be heading toward the Red," said Fiona. "Better than the Brazos." She glanced at Bone and Loraine. "Let's go check on your firearms at Newly's, shall we?"

"Waitin' on me, you're backin' up, gra...uh, Fiona," said Bone.

She gave him a puzzled look before turning and heading toward the gun shop.

TRAIN DEPOT
PARIS, TEXAS

The six man Paris Brass Band struck up a rousing rendition of John Philip Sousa's, *The Stars and Stripes Forever,* as the KATY train from St. Louis chugged into the station.

The town's mayor and other officials dressed in their top hats and other finery, waited patiently on the red brick platform for the steps from the passenger cars to be set in place.

They all turned their faces as the engineer in the big 4x4x2 coal-fired locomotive cab released the pressure from the boilers. The huge white cloud of steam rapidly disbursed in the morning breeze.

BONE

The mayor waved to the band to stop playing. He stepped forward to the private passenger car's steps as a mustachioed 5' 9", barrel-chested, stocky man wearing khaki jodhpurs, tall riding boots, a pencil-roll brim Stetson, and a khaki jacket, belted at the waist, stepped down. The mayor grinned big and stuck out his hand.

"Welcome to Paris, Texas, Mister Assistant Secretary Roosevelt...I do hope your trip was pleasant...I'm Mayor Buford Steiner."

"A bully trip as could be expected, Mister Stiener...as could be expected. Got to see a lot of this beautiful country...A bully trip indeed."

Several of his entourage followed him down the four metal steps from the car including his gun bearer carrying several long leather cases containing Theodore's hunting rifles.

Teddy himself, had a closed flap style holster containing a double-action M1892 Army .38 Long Colt revolver strapped around his hips.

A bent, stoop-shouldered colored man with a tow sack and a three foot piece of hoe handle with a sharpened nail driven in one end, shuffled around the platform picking up trash.

Tarlton Brewster, the tall, slender, rough-dressed gunhawk, rolled a quirly under a large red oak at the side of the depot as he watched the proceedings. He pulled a Lucifer from his vest pocket, struck it with his thumbnail, and lit the twisted end of the smoke.

Brewster and the equally rough-dressed heavyset, thick-necked gunman beside him watched three more of Roosevelt's group disembark the train, each carrying luggage.

They nodded at each another and sauntered toward their horses tied to a hitch rail down in front of the depot.

A bearded man wearing jeans, a greasy buckskin shirt and a floppy old cavalry campaign hat walked up to Roosevelt and stuck out a grimy hand.

"Mister Roosevelt, I'm Possum Middens, yer huntin' guide."

Theodore glanced at the man over his wire-rimmed C-bridge type pince-nez glasses perched on his nose.

The mayor gave the rank smelling woodsman a condescending look that would melt steel. "Please wait until we have finished our welcome for the Assistant Secretary, if you would…Mister

Middens." He moved his ample bulk in between the odiferous man and Theodore.

"Give us a few moments, my good man, if you would...You may see to the luggage and firearms my people are carrying," said Roosevelt.

Possum spat a long stream of viscous tobacco juice off to the side splattering it on the bricks and wiped his mouth with his sleeve. "Whatever you say, squire." He turned and headed toward the group of men standing nearby, still congregated at the bottom of the steps of the plush railcar.

"You fellers foller me with them bags an' yer traps. Got a wagon over yonder," he shouted, drowning out the mayor's spiel.

The colored custodian eased toward the corner of the depot, deposited his partially filled sack in a trash barrel and stepped inside the building.

In a few moments a tall, straight black cowboy walked out of the front of the depot and toward a sixteen hand gray stallion tied to a hitching rail down the street a short distance. He mounted and followed the two gunhawks as they walked their horses to the other side of the wagon.

"Easier'n I thought, Bull, eliminatin' that huntin' crew an' guide, an' replacin' 'em with our'n," said Tarlton.

"Yeah, gittin' that pompous bastard when Possum gits 'im out of town an' across the Red an' up into the Kiamichis will be like startin' a fire with kerosene," commented the other gunhawk, Bull Weaver.

"When will the Roosevelt group get up into the Nations?" asked a suave dark-haired, blue-eyed Castilian Spaniard sitting in front of the boss.

The portly, well-dressed man across the hand-carved desk from him, raised up, leaned forward with a bottle of wine and filled the Spaniard's long-stemmed crystal wine glass.

"1873…A prime vintage, Don Miguel…And to answer your question, the Kiamichi Mountains are around eighty miles from here. They should arrive at the Seven Devil Hills in three to four days."

"Why are we waiting until they get there, *amigo*?" Don Miguel swirled and sniffed the wine glass under his nose, and then took a sip.

"The Seven Devil Hills area in the Kiamichis are a true wilderness. There have been numerous people to enter…and never to be heard of again."

Ambassador Don Miguel Fernández, of Spain, nodded. *"Muy bueno, amigo, muy bueno.* Prime Minister Antonio Cánovas Del Castillo will be most pleased." He took another sip. "Most pleased, indeed."

§§§

CHAPTER SEVEN

NEWLY'S GUN SHOP
JACKSBORO, TEXAS

The two inch brass doorbell attached to the header by a strap of spring steel tinkled as Bone, Fiona and Loraine entered the small shop.

"Mornin', folks," said Newly looking up from his work table. "Right on time...Just puttin' the finishin' touches on Loraine's gunbelt."

He laid Bone's belt with the 500 in the holster on the counter along with several boxes of .50 caliber shells, and then Loraine's.

Newly opened a box of new .45 caliber smokeless rounds he had made for her and filled the twenty loops he had sewed on the belt after putting the three sleeves for her magazines on. Both belts also included sheaths for their Bowie knives.

"Good golly, Newly, this is nice...Damn nice," said Bone as he picked up the belt and pistol.

"Strap it on. Let's see how it fits...You too, Loraine," commented Newly.

They both did as he suggested, slipped the weapons out and dropped them back in several times.

"Stop by Sewell's, get some butter an' work it on the inside of the holsters every few days for the next week or so. It'll loosen them up an' mold to the shape...The guns'll be less likely to stick."

"Better'n neatsfoot oil?" asked Bone.

"For the inside of the bucket, yes. Use neatsfoot oil for the rest just like on a saddle...Butter is also better for the finish of the guns than the oil."

"Wow, these are great...What do we owe you?" asked Loraine.

"Oh, fifteen dollars apiece'll cover it, I reckon," he replied. "That includes the ammo."

"Dang, that's all?" asked an incredulous Bone.

Newly grinned. "Considerin' the fact I got to fire each one, it was a pleasure workin' on 'em...A real pleasure...Let's go out back an' ya'll can try your trigger pulls...Worked on 'em some." He winked and grinned again.

"Great," replied Loraine after she buckled the gunbelt around her hips and snugged it into place. "Should we get some rawhide thongs to tie them down to our legs?"

"What for?" asked Fiona.

"Don't the gunfighters do that to speed up their draw?" replied Loraine.

Fiona and Newly exchanged confused glances.

The marshal shook her head. "Never seen anyone do that. The general idea is to hit what you're shooting at, not how fast you can draw."

"What was it Wyatt Earp said?...'Fast is fine, but accuracy is final'," added Newly.

"Think it's the movie cowboys and the re-enactors that do that in our time, Pard. They aren't usin' live ammo or have anybody shootin' back at 'em," said Bone.

"Movie actors?" asked Newly.

"Like play actors...performers," replied Fiona.

"Ah...Well, none the less, who would I have to kill to get handguns like these?" Newly inquired facetiously.

Bone arched his eyebrows and smiled. "Probably us."

"Oh...right." He smiled back.

Out back of Newly's shop, they stepped up to a line of railroad ties on the ground facing a stack of hay bales thirty-five feet away. There were several twelve-inch wide planks of white pine, with black circles four-inches in diameter in the center, propped against the hay.

"Pick one." Newly pointed at the boards. He handed them wads of cotton each. "Here, you'll need this." He poked a small ball into each ear.

Fiona, Loraine and Bone followed suit.

Bone put his toes close to the ties, drew the 500 and squeezed off three rounds.

After the echoes of the tremendous explosions from the .50 cal died, they looked at Bone's board.

There were two holes inside the black ring. One hole was a little larger than the other showing two rounds virtually on top of each other. The third round was less than a quarter-inch away.

"Sorry, the first one was a little off. Not used to that light of a trigger pull...but, I love it," exclaimed Bone. "All right, Pard, your turn."

Loraine stepped up to the line, smoothly pulled her Kimber from its holster and fired three times that sounded like one continuous roar. There was one large, oddly shaped hole in the center of her black circle.

"Nice shootin', Pard," complimented Bone.

"Wow, wow, wow...is all I can say." She glanced at her 1911 semiautomatic. "The trigger pull is awesome...Must be down to three pounds."

"Two point eight to be exact, Loraine," replied Newly.

"My, my." She shook her head in wonder.

"May I try?" asked Fiona.

"Sure," replied Bone as he reloaded his 500 and handed it to her. "Remember, it's double action...Just squeeze the trigger."

She glanced at him. "I know."

The last word just left her lips as the .50 roared with an almost continuous explosion—there was one hole in her board like Loraine's, but bigger.

"Holy cow," exclaimed Bone as she handed him his pistol back and took Loraine's Kimber from her.

"Nice kick to it, but not bad," commented Fiona.

She racked the slide like Loraine had shown her, instantly squeezed off three rounds from the .45, and like Loraine, there was only one sound—and one hole. "Oh, my stars. That's unbelievable."

"Uh, better ease that hammer back down, Fiona, and safe the weapon…there's still a live round in the chamber and the hammer's in the cocked position."

"Oh, right." She had a sheepish grin on her face.

"You'll also notice I didn't have to reload," commented Loraine. "There's still two rounds left after you and I both fired…Now watch this." She took the weapon back from Fiona.

Loraine pushed the release button allowing the magazine to drop out to the ground, racked the slide to eject the round in the chamber. She then pulled a full magazine from her belt, slipped it into the empty chamber in the grip and popped it on the bottom with the heel of her hand, seating it. A quick rack of the slide chambered the first round.

Loraine glanced at Fiona and Newly. "Fully reloaded…Less than two seconds. I can fire sixteen rounds in five seconds." She grinned. "But, you won't want to touch the barrel for a little bit…That's an extreme example, though."

"Gets a bit warmish, I would imagine," commented Fiona. "I expect some doeskin gloves would help."

"That's a good idea," replied Loraine with a nod.

"Well I would say let's go pack up. We'll have to go horse and muleback to Gainesville to get to the train…We can stop and spend the night at the Wilson ranch," said Fiona.

"Wonderful, love to see Lucy and the Wilsons again." Bone stuck out his hand to Newly. "You did a hellova job, sir. Can't tell you how much we appreciate it."

"Anytime…It was a pleasure working on those weapons. Let me clean and tune 'em up when ya'll get back," he replied.

"We keep them pretty clean, Newly. Have to in our business," said Loraine.

He nodded. "Can understand that. But, I'll take 'em completely apart...Noticed that usin' that smokeless powder doesn't leave near as much residue as black powder...and I suspect almost no pitting in the barrel."

"Think that was one of the reasons they came up with it," said Bone.

"Not counting the fact that there's no telltale white smoke cloud for the bad guys to shoot back at," added Fiona.

"Point," agreed Bone. "Well, catch you on the flip side, Newly." He stuck out his hand.

"Flip side?...Flip side of what?" He looked puzzled.

Bone ducked his head and grinned. "When we get back, I mean."

"Oh, sure thing," Newly replied as he shook Bone's ham-like hand.

The three turned and headed up a cross alley back to the main street.

"Meet ya'll at Mom's," said Bone.

"Where you going?" asked Loraine.

"Newspaper office."

JACK COUNTY, TEXAS

Flynn and Newton trotted along to the north following the tracks of the escaped outlaw. They were nearing the ridge escarpment south of the Red River when Newton stopped and growled, focusing his attention on the ridge.

The sheriff's head shot up as he scanned the scattered limestone boulders along the base of the prehistoric waterline carved by an ancient ocean from the late Cretaceous-Paleogene Period some 65 to 75 million years ago.

"Uh, oh…" he exclaimed, whipping Laddie's head around to duck into a copse of wild plum trees just as he heard the sickening thwack of a bullet striking flesh followed a half-second later by the boom of a rifle.

Laddie's shrill, woman-like, anguished scream from the pain and shock pierced the morning air as he collapsed to the ground on his right side. The thrashing of the mortally wounded gelding momentarily pinned Flynn's leg beneath his body as several other rounds smacked into the dirt around them.

BONE

Mason finally got his .45-70 long barreled 1895 Marlin pulled from its boot and—with his leg still trapped under Laddie—snapped off five quick rounds at the ball of white gunsmoke on the ridge two hundred yards away. He spread his fire over a six foot side-to-side pattern.

The gunshots stopped as the distant gunsmoke slowly drifted away on the light morning breeze. Flynn watched the spot for a couple of moments, and then started trying to pull his trapped leg from underneath the groaning Laddie.

Flynn finally succeeded in extracting his leg and paused for a short minute, to catch his breath, and then rolled over and examined his faithful mount.

"Aw, Jesus…" he whispered as the tears began to roll down his cheeks. "…lung shot…both of them, through and through."

The magnificent animal's breath came out in a bloody froth from his nostrils as he moaned in pain and vainly tried to breathe.

Mason cradled Laddie's head in his lap for what seemed like an hour, but was really only a couple of minutes as his body shook with silent sobs and he talked softly and soothingly to him, "Now I lay me down to sleep…I pray the Lord my soul to keep…May the angels watch me through the night…and keep me in their blessed sight…."

He then stood up and muttered in a low voice, "…My…my responsibility to…do what has to be…done." Mason tried to wipe the tears from his face, but it didn't do any good.

Newton lay beside the pair, his head between his front paws with his eyes knowingly on his master.

Mason's voice cracked slightly as he gently stroked Laddie's neck and his tears fell into the beautiful animal's black mane, "I'm…I'm so, so sorry, son…God knows that I am."

The gelding looked up at Flynn with his limpid soft brown eyes.

"I know it hurts…I know, son…You've always been…been my best pal…Please, please forgive me…I love you, boy," he whispered softly as he kissed the blue roan's cheek before he drew his Colt and placed the muzzle behind Laddie's ear…

§§§

CHAPTER EIGHT

COOKE COUNTY, TEXAS

The sun was settling toward the western horizon as Fiona, Loraine and Bone rode up to the white picket fence surrounding the front yard of the Wilson's well-kept ranch.

Lucy was sitting on the top step to the wraparound front porch of the large dog-run style ship lap white house with her arms wrapped around her knees. Her blond and white pit bull terrier, Garin, sat beside her.

"Hey, Lucy, how long have you been sittin' there?" asked Bone from outside the fence.

The childlike alien with brown pixie-cut hair got to her feet and ran to the front gate. "About two hours when I sensed you were crossing the Cooke County line headed this way."

Lucy stepped through the spring-loaded gate and gave Bone a big hug as he dismounted from his bay gelding. She also gave Fiona and Loraine hugs.

"You knew we were coming?" asked Loraine.

Lucy smiled. "Of course. I knew when you left Jacksboro…May I see that clipping, Bone?"

He reached into his saddlebags, retrieved a book, opened and pulled out a newspaper clipping. "Got you a new book to read, too, Mark Twain's *Adventures of Huckleberry Finn.*" He handed her the clipping.

"What's that?" asked Loraine as she tried to get a look at the paper.

"It's the article about Lucy's spacecraft crash at Aurora that appeared in the *Dallas Morning News* on April 19, 1897 two days after the crash…Thought she might like it."

BONE

Lucy gazed at the article and began to read:

"'*Dallas Morning News*, April 19, 1897' "...the by-line is a gentleman named S.E. Haydon... '*Space Craft Crashes Near Aurora, Texas...Pilot Killed...* '"

Lucy pursed her lips and paused as her eyes filled with tears and then continued, "... '*Aurora, Wise County, Texas, April 17, 1897...About 6 o'clock this morning the early risers of Aurora were astonished at the sudden appearance of the airship which has been sailing around the country. It was traveling due north and much nearer the earth than before. Evidently some of the machinery was out of order, for it was making a speed of only ten or twelve miles an hour, and gradually settling*

83

toward the earth. It sailed over the public square and when it reached the north part of town it collided with the tower of Judge Proctor's windmill and went into pieces with a terrific explosion, scattering debris over several acres of ground, wrecking the windmill and water tank and destroying the judge's flower garden. The pilot of the ship is supposed to have been the only one aboard and, while his remains were badly disfigured..."

Lucy stopped again and wiped her eyes, as her adoptive parents, Cletus and Mary Lou Wilson, stepped out of the green painted gingerbread screen door from the house—Mary Lou was Mason Flynn's sister. Lucy took a deep breath and her voice softened, "*...enough of the original has been picked up to show that he was not an inhabitant of this world... 'Mr. T.J. Weems, the US Army Signal Service officer at this place and an authority on astronomy, gives it as his opinion that the pilot was a native of the planet Mars'.*"

Lucy couldn't help but get a small grin on her cherub-like face at that line. She shook her head and continued to read, "*'Papers found on his person—evidently the records of his travels—are written in some unknown hieroglyphics and cannot be deciphered. The ship was too badly wrecked to form any conclusion as to its construction or motive power. It was built of an unknown metal, resembling somewhat a mixture of aluminum and silver, and it must have weighed several tons. The town is today full of people who are viewing the wreckage and gathering specimens of strange metal from the debris. The pilot's funeral will take place tomorrow'."*

Lucy glanced around at everyone and wiped the tears from her antique gold eyes with the back of her fingers again.

"I stayed in the shadow of a large tree next to the cemetery in my invisible mode while they performed the burial ceremony of my mate, Garin...They were very considerate and I thank them for that."

Lucy reached up as Bone bent over to her 4' 10" height and hugged his neck again. "And thank you Bone, for bringing this to me...and for the book. I love you."

"I love you, too, Lucy." He turned away to wipe his own eyes.

Mary Lou dabbed her eyes with a dishtowel she had in her hands. "Well, Cletus, if you'll help Mister Bone with the horses, us ladies will go set the table. Got a big bowl of chicken 'n dumplin's and buttermilk cornbread for supper."

"Thought I smelled somethin' good when we rode up...and it's just plain Bone, Mary Lou," he said with a grin.

She slapped her thigh with the dishtowel. "I know. It's just so darned hard since it's so descriptive."

"Can't help it. It was my daddy's family name...Got it by default." He grinned big as he and Cletus led the horses and Fiona's mule, Spot, toward the barn.

Everyone sat in chairs or on the steps of the front porch in the gloaming after dinner, enjoying a cup of coffee.

"That was an outstanding supper, Mary Lou, especially the peach cobbler," said Fiona.

"Oh, pshaw It was just something I threw together."

"Uh, huh…I could get a degree from a culinary school and not come up with anything close to that, Mary Lou," commented Loraine.

"Yeah, you know how long it took you to learn to make coffee at the office, Pard," replied Bone.

"Had too, Bone, that paint remover you were making when I came on board was giving everyone the trots."

"Beggars can't be choosers," said Bone as he took a sip of his coffee and leaned back in the slat-back rocker.

"To change the subject, Lucy, you never mentioned what you and your mate were doing here when you crashed," asked Fiona.

She smiled and glanced at the tall, statuesque woman. "Well, it's about a two million year old story…You see, my race…what the Sumerians called the *Anunnaki*…are what are known throughout the galaxy as *Watchers*."

"What do you mean, *Watchers*, Lucy?" asked Cletus.

"*Watchers* would be synonymous with *Protectors*, Papa…We have been protecting your world for millennia. There are other alien races in this galaxy who are...well, let's say, not as benevolent as the *Anunnaki*..."

"Like the Reptiods?" interrupted Bone.

"Like the Reptiods...Our fleet was in a great battle with the Reptiod fleet out near the Mars orbit. They were on the way to Terra...that's what we call Earth...to subjugate your people and turn them into one of their prime suppliers of protein..."

"She means we would be their cattle," interrupted Bone again. "Loraine and I fought some of their ships that made it past the *Anunnaki* in 2014 with a secret group called the Black Eagle Force...and Lucy." — *"Black Eagle Force: Invasion" – 2014*

"We were to be their food source?" asked an incredulous Mary Lou.

"In a word...Yes," answered Bone. "...We're still here...they aren't"

"Yes, it was close, but, we managed to drive them off again. But, in last year in 1897, my mate, Garin, and I were piloting a small fighter craft in the battle near Mars. We took a grazing hit from one of their energy weapons that knocked our interstellar drive out and sent us spinning toward Earth."

"That's when you crashed?" added Fiona.

Lucy nodded. "As was reported in the newspaper article...the pilot, my mate Garin, was killed...I managed to survive...somehow."

"That's when Mason and I found her and brought her to his sister Mary Lou and her husband, Cletus...They pretend that she's an abandoned child and adopted her." Fiona nodded toward the pair.

"According to Bone and Loraine, I'll be here until 2014 before I'm rescued by my people...You see there's not really much difference between us and you Americans...just on a smaller scale."

"How so, Lucy?" asked Bone.

"There are countries on your world that try to subjugate other, smaller countries, for their own benefit," said Lucy.

"Yes, like Spain is trying to keep Cuba under their monarchy or dictatorship just off our shores...if you will," added Fiona.

"Something like that," replied Lucy.

"There are numerous politicians in Washington that are pushing for the US to attack the Spanish and drive them back to Spain...That's why the United States government is going to be sending our newest battleship, USS Maine, down to

Havana…To let Spain know they're not welcome in this hemisphere…in this time frame," commented Bone. "A show of force…so to speak. The current Assistant Secretary of the Navy, Theodore Roosevelt, has been quoted as saying, 'Speak softly, but carry a big stick'."

"How do you know that?" asked Fiona.

Bone raised his right eyebrow at her.

"Oh…right," said Fiona.

Lucy looked at Bone and smiled.

§§§

CHAPTER NINE

JACK COUNTY, TEXAS

Flynn closed Laddie's eyes softly with his hand. Newton nuzzled up to him and softly kissed the side of his face. Flynn rubbed the top of the faithful dog's head. "Thanks, boy."

He got slowly to his feet, pulled his saddlebags free, slung them over his shoulder, looked down at his horse for a long moment, and then took a deep breath. "I'm goin' to get that son of a bitch, Laddie…I can promise you that…He's gonna pay."

Without looking back again, he strode with a purpose and fire in his sky blue eyes toward the ridge in the distance with Newton padding alongside. He didn't care if he was making himself a target or not.

Flynn stopped briefly to remove his boots and don his Apache style moccasins, and then headed directly to the spot where he had seen the cloud of gunsmoke.

He and Newton worked their way through the boulders that looked like a child had gotten angry and scattered his toy blocks about.

The Indian footwear enabled him to clamber over many of the rocks without the danger of slipping like with his slick-soled boots.

Halfway up the ridge he came to the spot where he had fixed his gaze. He scouted around a bit before he noticed several brass casings between two large boulders.

".45-60…Most likely a '76 Winchester…Well, what's this, boy?" He knelt down at a brown area in the sand. "Blood...Got a piece of the bastard," he muttered. "Let's see how bad."

Flynn first checked the area of the ridge above him closely, and then tracked the blood spatter trail through the jumbled rocks like he'd learned from Loraine.

"Leg hit...draggin' his left. Fell...Staggered back up." *Keep alert, Flynn, a wounded animal is the most dangerous.* He mused.

Mason drew his Colt as he crept up the ridge. After a few dozen feet, he heard a moan. He eared back the hammer on his .45 and nodded to Newton.

The dog crawled on his belly up to a broken chunk of limestone the size of a wagon and peered around the side. He got to his feet and woofed back at Flynn, who stepped forward.

"Please help me," came a plea from the wounded outlaw.

He had wrapped his wild rag around his thigh, but it had already bled through. There was also a wound in his upper stomach with blood soaking his shirt and trousers. His Winchester was still in his hand.

Mason reached down, picked the rifle up and smashed it against the boulder, and then removed the Remington from his holster.

"Please...please help me," he pleaded again.

"Why? You sorry sack of shit...You tried to kill me."

"Naw, naw...No way...I was shootin' at yer horse...Figured you couldn't chase me...shanks mare."

Flynn gritted his teeth and hissed, "That's even worse, you scum...suckin'...pig."

"Are you gonna help me 'for I bleed to death?"

Mason stared at him for a long moment before answering, "Nope...don't believe I will."

"For God's sake, Sheriff...I'm gut shot."

Flynn got a wry grin. "Yeah...I know...Where's your horse?"

"Just...just over the top of the ridge, why?"

"I need somethin' to ride, stupid."

"What?...You just gonna leave me here to die?"

Mason nodded. "That's the plan...You horse shootin' son of a bitch...But, tell you what do..."

He shucked the shells from the man's Remington, threw all but one back down the slope, and then unbuckled his gunbelt, jerked it off and threw it down after them.

"What's your name?" asked Flynn.

"Bert, Bert McLain."

"Yeah, seen dodgers on you…Thief, murderer, rapist. You're a nice feller, ain'tcha?…Worth a thousand dollars…dead or alive. But, you know what, asswagon?…I don't care."

Mason placed the empty pistol ten feet away uphill, and then the single .44-40 round another twenty feet more toward the top. "There you are, horse killer…Yours if you can get to 'em…Enjoy your stay in Hell," he said over his shoulder as he and Newton started climbing their way on up to the top.

"It ain't fair! Yer a lawman!…You gotta take me in…You cain't do this," McLain screamed as he watched Flynn disappear around a boulder.

"Watch me," came the steely voice back.

Mason climbed his way to the top and found McLain's horse tethered to a scrub cedar. He stroked the grulla gelding on the side of the neck, inserted his Marlin in the empty boot and checked the cinch.

"Worthless bastard didn't even bother to loosen your girth so you could catch your breath after climbin' this ridge."

He stabbed his foot in the stirrup and swung easily into the saddle. Flynn nudged the horse toward a more gentle slope of the ridge to go back down.

The trio had worked almost halfway toward the bottom of the steep ridge face when Mason heard a single pistol shot echo through the boulders.

"Huh…Made it quicker'n I thought, Newt," he said as they reached the bottom. "Well, horse, guess we better go get my saddle an' chunk this piece of crap…Don't fit you anyway. Then we'll pitch camp…Already gettin' dark."

WILSON RANCH

The sun was hiding just below the horizon and was already casting a mixture of red, yellow and orange streaks on the horizon into the blue velvet of the night to the west.

Fiona looked to the east as she was snugging up her cinch on her painted mule, Spot. "'Wake! For the Sun, who scatter'd into flight the Stars before him from the Field of Night, Drives Night along with them from Heav'n, and strikes the Sultan's Turret with a Shaft of Light'."

"Who said that?" asked Bone as he tied his saddlebags behind his cantle.

"Omar Khayyám."

Bone glanced back up to the porch at the morning glory flowers in the beds on either side of the steps, and then back at the glow to the east. "When you arise in the morning, think of what a precious privilege it is to be alive...to breathe, to think, to enjoy...to love."

Fiona glanced at the big man in surprise. "Marcus Aurelius."

Bone nodded. "It was one of my grandmother's favorite quotes...Got it from her mother."

"How interesting...it's one of mine also," Fiona replied.

"You don't say," he replied with a wry grin.

Lucy walked through the gate in the white picket fence to the hitching rails. "Bone, you and Loraine might consider contacting *Anompoli Lawa*. He may have some information about your portal."

"Who?" asked Loraine.

"Doctor Winchester Ashalatubbi. He's the medical doctor and Shaman for the Chickasaw Nation," answered Fiona. "Very smart man. He's well versed in Indian myths, legends and lore."

"Really? How cool. My grandfather was half Chickasaw," commented Bone.

"We can send him a telegram in Ardmore when we get to Gainesville…It's possible he might can meet us in Paris…He knows Bass well," said Fiona. "We should be at Faye's boarding house in Gainesville about noon," said Fiona. "The next train east to Paris won't be until tomorrow morning."

They exchanged hugs with Lucy and the Wilsons and mounted up.

"Mason could be coming through in a day or two after he takes care of that outlaw he had to go chase down," added Fiona. "He'll be joining up with us either in Gainesville or Paris."

"We'll feed my baby brother and send him on his way," said Mary Lou.

The first rays of sunlight reached the group trotting toward the road as the big yellow orb was peeking halfway up from the eastern horizon and rapidly pushing the night to the west.

Lucy smiled and watched them disappear around the bend of the road. "He hasn't told Mason and Fiona yet."

"Told them what, Lucy?" asked Mary Lou.

"That he's their great grandson."

Mary Lou put her hand to her mouth. "Oh, my…" She glanced at Cletus. "Guess that makes him our great grand nephew…in the future."

"Son of a gun…It would appear so."

PARIS, TEXAS

The afternoon sun was beating through the window panes at the end of the hall when an old bent colored man with a homemade cane, rapped on the six paneled door of room 6 of the Red River Hotel. The door was opened by a mustachioed, bespeckled, stocky, forty-year old man.

"Yes, how may I help you?"

The messenger snatched his battered old fedora from his close-cropped nappy head. "Has a message fer a Massa Rooo-se-velt…He be heah?"

"Roosevelt...I'm Theodore Roosevelt, what is it?"

"Don't know, Massa, cain't read." The black man handed him a sealed yellow envelope.

Roosevelt took the telegram and gave him a Morgan silver dollar.

"Lawdamercy!...Thankee, thankee kindly, sir," the colored messenger exclaimed as he looked at the silver coin, and then slipped it into his coat pocket.

He nodded at Roosevelt several times, shoved his hat back on his head and, leaning on his cane, shuffled back down the hallway.

The colored man glanced back over his shoulder to make sure the door had closed, entered the next room on his right and closed the door behind him.

He propped his cane against the wall, put both hands behind his back straightened up, groaning slightly and grinned.

"Gittin' harder an' harder to do that."

"What's that? The bending over part or the straightening up part?" asked the Secret Service agent, reclining on one of the two beds in the room.

"Both."

BONE

The black man strode purposely across the room to the wash basin and filled the tumbler sitting on the dresser from the pitcher and took a long drink.

"Gittin' close to time," he said.

"It is…It is, indeed, Bass…When do you expect Marshal Miller?" asked agent Wesley Thomas.

"Reckon tomorrow…an' it's Marshal Flynn now. Got herself married to a warhorse of a lawman from down to Jacksboro way…Sheriff Mason Flynn…One tough *nakni'*."

"What's a *nakni'*?"

"Chickasaw for 'man'," said Bass.

"Why didn't you say so?"

"Just did."

§§§

CHAPTER TEN

SKEANS BOARDING HOUSE
GAINESVILLE, TEXAS

Fiona, Bone and Loraine climbed the six steps to the twelve foot wide wraparound porch on the front of the red brick Queen Anne style three story Victorian house.

She opened the green painted gingerbread screen door, and then the white ornate glass centered main door and entered the foyer.

"Faye? Anybody home?" she shouted.

The dark-blonde-haired owner of the boarding house burst through the door at the end of the foyer from the kitchen, wiping her hands on a dishtowel. "Fiona! I'd recognize that voice anywhere."

She hugged the tall woman's neck, and then she noticed Bone and Loraine behind her.

"My Lord in Heaven," the five-foot two inch woman said as she looked up. "Who are these folks? Where's Babe, your big blue ox?...You have to be Paul Bunyon and his wife, Lucette."

They both laughed.

"Close enough, Faye...I'm Bone and this is my partner, Loraine."

"Partner?" she asked.

"They're police officers...uh, from out of town," offered Fiona. "This is Faye Skeans. She owns the boarding house.

Bone removed his John Bull hat and bowed slightly. "Pleased, Ma'am." He glanced at Fiona. "I can call *her* Ma'am, can't I?"

"You'd better," said Faye as she took his hat and hung it on a hall tree. "Come in, come in. Lunch is almost ready...Pot roast."

"Oh, my favorite," said Fiona.

A beautiful 5' 8" waspwaisted blond with clear blue eyes stepped gracefully down the stairs with a boy and girl two and a half year old cotton-headed children holding on to each hand.

"Fiona!" she squealed.

"Annabel!" responded Fiona. "And would you look at those babies."

The two women embraced while the male child toddled over and tugged on Bone's pant leg.

"Up," he said.

Bone bent over and lifted the boy up to his eye level. "And who are you?"

"Me Bass." He looked down. "Cassie…sissy."

"I can tell," said Bone as he rolled Bass into his left arm and picked up his fraternal twin sister, Cassie Ann, in his right.

"They both love to be picked up…I swear, gettin' almost too big for me to lift," Annabel said in her musical Alabama lilt. "They were named after Bass Reeves…He was the one mainly responsible for delivering them."

"Looky here, looky here," came a voice from the top of the stairway. "That's a Special Deputy US Marshal Fiona Mae Flynn if I ever saw one," said the tall, rawboned, redheaded, freckled-faced man strolling down the stairs. "Who's man mountain here and his lady friend?"

"I wouldn't go that far," quipped Loraine.

"This is Detective D. U. Bone and his partner, Inspector Loraine Rodriguez," answered Fiona.

"What does the D. U. stand for?" asked Bodie.

"My given name of Darrell Ulysses, but..."

"Damn You, is what it has come to actually mean," interjected Loraine quickly.

Bone shrugged and arched his right eyebrow.

"Why is that?" asked a puzzled Bodie Hickman.

"If you're around him long enough, you'll understand," Loraine said with a smile.

"Thanks Double D...tell everything you know," commented Bone, looking at her bosom.

"Damn you, Bone." She glanced at the others. "See?"

"They do this all the time," commented Fiona.

"If anything unusual happens and Bone is around or has been around...don't bother asking who did it," said Loraine.

"Guess you're going to say me?" replied Bone.

"I suppose it wasn't you that mixed the gunpowder from two 12 gauge shotgun shells in an ashtray in our Chief of Police's office just before the Sheriff came in."

"I don't understand," said Faye.

Loraine glanced at Bone again. "You see, the sheriff always had a cigarette or cigar in his hand...and when he came in the office, he would stub it out in the chief's ashtray..."

"You didn't?" interrupted Fiona turning to Bone.

"He did...All we could hear through the smoke boiling down the hall was the sheriff screaming, 'Damn you, Bone!...You burnt me up.'...Singed off his eyebrows, and eyelashes...plus all the hair from his hands and arms."

All eyes went to Bone.

He shrugged again. "Seemed like the thing to do at the time."

"Hey, I gotta remember that," said Ranger Hickman.

"You do an' I'll snatch you baldheaded, mister...bless your heart," said Annabel.

"Enough of this. Ya'll go wash up. I'm going to set lunch on the table," said Faye. "Have ya'll seen to your horses?"

"We fed and watered them around back in the carriage house and washed up at the bench beside the well before we came in," said Fiona.

"Good girl," replied Faye.

"Didn't you say Brushy Bill Roberts stayed here too, Fiona?" asked Bone.

"He's up in the Arbuckles workin' with Marshal McGann on a rustlin' case or somethin'," commented Bodie.

"That's Bass' old partner," said Bone.

"Yep...but don't let him hear you call him old," added Bodie. "He's purty salty...He's also my godfather."

"What are ya'll doing over this way?" asked Faye as they made their way into the dining room.

"Got a telegram from the Office of the United States Marshal asking me to meet Bass in Paris on a case involving the Secret Service and the US Marshal Office," Fiona replied.

"Secret Service, too?...Sounds like you're goin' to need the Texas Rangers in on this," said Bodie.

"My thoughts exactly," she answered.

"And Bone and Loraine?" Bodie asked, and then looked at the guns in the holsters strapped around the two law officers. "What in the Sam Hill are those?"

Bone and Loraine exchanged glances with Fiona.

"Might as well tell them...they're family," said Fiona.

"Tell us what?" asked Faye as she turned before heading into the kitchen.

"Well, you see, Ma'am, we don't really belong here," offered Loraine.

"Excuse me?" asked Annabel.

"What she means..." Bone looked at Loraine. "...we're from here...but we're not from this time."

"I don't understand at all," said a puzzled Faye as she looked at Fiona.

"Me neither," added Annabel.

"Or me," commented Bodie.

"We're, uh...from the future," said Loraine.

Annabel began fanning her face with her hand. "Oh, my...think I'm gettin' the vapors."

Bodie quickly pulled out a chair from the dining table for his wife to sit down. She gathered the children next to her.

"Did we hear you correctly, Loraine?" asked Faye.

"Yes, ma'am, you did. If we all go ahead and sit down, we'll fill you in," said Bone as he pulled out a chair for Loraine, and then he took the one next to her.

Fifteen minutes later, Bone finished telling how they came to be here through an ancient Indian portal down next to the Brazos, and everything that had happened so far. "...and well, that's the name of that tune."

"Oh, my, my, my...Maybe I should go ahead and bring the pot roast and fixings in before it gets cold," said Faye as she got to her feet.

"Don't think I'd believe any of this if we didn't already know Lucy an' her story...The fact that you know her from your time is..."

"I do declare...I am completely flummoxed," commented Annabel, interrupting Bodie.

"Lucy suggested we contact Doctor Ashalatubbi...said he might have some answers for us...There has to be more than one reason we're here," said Bone as he glanced hungrily at the large pot roast Faye had just set on the table.

"One of them was probably you taking that bullet for Fiona," said Loraine.

"Maybe he was making sure it wasn't my time yet." She glanced at the big man. "We sent a couple of telegrams when we got to town, before we came over here," said Fiona. "One to Winchester and the other to the Office of the US Marshal in Washington giving them an update and when we should arrive in Paris."

"By the way, why isn't Mason with ya'll?" asked Bodie.

"He had to chase down a miscreant...One of four that tried to rob Barber's Mercantile, in Jacksboro," answered Fiona.

"What about the other three?" Faye asked.

"They committed suicide by cop," answered Bone, without looking up, as he filled his plate with roast, potatoes and gravy.

"Suicide by...Oh, my goodness," said Annabel bringing her hand to her mouth.

"He'll be joinin' us as soon as he can," said Fiona.

"I'm sure he'll be by." Faye looked at Fiona and smiled. "When is it?"

"When is wha..." she blushed. "How did you..."

"Fiona, honey, I knew the moment you came in the door."

"You mean you're…" jumped in Annabel.

Fiona nodded. "About two months, I'm guessing."

"You haven't been to the doctor?" asked Annabel.

"Hasn't been time," answered Fiona.

"What are ya'll talkin' about?" asked Bone as he buttered a hot yeast roll.

Loraine kicked him under the table. "She's pregnant, doofus."

Bone almost choked on the tea he had just taken a swallow of. Instead, a little dribbled out of his nose. "Oh, Lordy, Lordy…You don't mean it?" He wiped his nose and upper lip with his napkin.

"What's the matter, Bone, didn't your mother ever have that talk with you?" asked Faye with a twinkle in her eye.

"Well, yessum, of course…it's just we may be going in harm's way and…"

"Bone, now you listen to me…It's just like I told Mason yesterday…I was chasing down malefactors long before I met him…I think I know when to back off." She put a large piece of roast on her plate.

"Boy howdy…sure hope so," Bone muttered.

"What was that?" Fiona looked daggers at him.

"Just said, "Boy howdy…sure is good pot roast."

"Uh, huh," Fiona replied, still staring at the big man and shaking her head. "You remind me so much of Mason."

Bone snorted tea from his nose again.

§§§

CHAPTER ELEVEN

GLOVES FORK CREEK
CHOCTAW NATION, IT

Tarlton Brewster wrapped his worn and faded blue neckerchief around the handle of the large coffee pot sitting on a flat rock next to the fire and filled his tin cup.

"Hey, Brewster, how 'bout some of that brew for me?" asked a half-breed Choctaw, Haywood

Tenkiller, one of the fifteen men sitting around the camp.

He chuckled at what he perceived as a joke as he leaned back against his saddle and held out his cup.

"Why don't you try out for a minstrel show…Hayseed?…And pour yer own damn coffee."

Brewster's collection of gunmen and outlaws had pitched camp in a glen bordering Gloves Fork Creek just southwest of the Seven Devils Hills and northeast of Doaksville. The creek was almost on a line from Paris, Texas to the Kiamichi wilderness.

"How's come we didn't jest stay at the cave, Brewster? Got all our stuff there," said Tobacca Bob Buckley as he spat on a log in the fire, creating a brief small steam cloud as it hissed away.

"Because, jackanape, it's over twenty miles from the route Possum is taking Roosevelt an' his nabobs to the Kiamichis," said Brewster. "Yer about two shots short of havin' a empty bottle, you know that?"

"Huh?…Ain't got no bottle, Brewster…Hey, yer a funnin' me, ain'tcha?"

"No flies on you, Tobacca," said Brewster as he blew across the top of his cup and took a sip.

"Naw, 'baccer keeps 'em away." He spat again.

"I kin believe it," muttered Brewster.

"What'er we gonna do onct we nab his lordship," asked Little Dime Williams.

"Then we go to the cave, to meet with the boss and that Spaniard dandy, jackwagon," said Brewster. "There's a pit way in the back there...Chunked a rock in it...Never did hear it hit the bottom."

"Damnation," said the gunslick, Bull Weaver.

"Well, I fer one am gittin' tired of jest sittin' round this camp an' drinkin' coffee," said Boone Prescott, a skinny-as-a-rail outlaw. "You'd think we'd have a little who-hit-John."

"Why don't you jump yer sorry ass up an' trundle into town an' git us some," said Ugly George McSween.

"How's 'bout you take a flyin' leap at my 'sorry ass', McSween," retorted Prescott.

Ugly George immediately got up and charged into Prescott. The two rolled about on the ground, punching, gouging and biting each other.

"Ow, ow, ow," screamed McSween. "Yer bitin' my leg...That ain't fair!"

Ugly George leaned over and grabbed Prescott's nose between his thumb and forefinger and twisted.

"Dang it, cut it out, McSween, that hurts," he said with a decided nasal twang as he twisted free.

"That's the point, asswipe," countered Ugly George. "Quit a bitin' me."

Most of the other men were now on their feet egging the two on and trading bets.

"Hey, are ya'll fightin' er makin' love?" asked Big Floyd Atkins.

"Meby they're dancin'" said Lane Doyle, a mustachioed stocky man walking back into camp from taking care of some business.

"I vote fer them makin' love," said Bull Weaver with a laugh.

"Yeah, they wuz both gittin' a mite ripe," added Bull.

George got to his feet and dragged Boone up also, only to get a haymaker across the side of his head. He tumbled back to the ground and had just rolled over when Prescott jumped on his back pummeling him with both fists.

Ugly George twisted over underneath Boone and grabbed him in a bear hug. The pair rolled over again and into the five foot deep water of the creek.

Prescott's face broke the surface, spitting water and shaking his head.

A panicked Ugly George also came to the surface thrashing both arms and screaming, "Cain't swim, cain't swim...Help, help! Don't let me drown."

Boone reached over and grabbed McSween by the hair and held his face up out of the water. "Put yer feet down, Ugly George, water ain't but 'bout five feet deep."

McSween stopped thrashing about and stood up. "Oh," he said with an embarrassed look on his face. "Didn't know."

"Now you do...," said Little Dime from the bank. "...next time ya'll roll into the creek." He cackled like a chicken.

"Ya'll oughta do that more often, McSween...Do believe it improved yer looks," said Tobacca Bob.

"Probably jest washed some of the dirt off," commented Tall Jim Reed.

"Well, suspect you ya-hoos is gonna git yer fill of fightin' in a few days, anyhoo," said Brewster. "Don't figure it's gonna be much of a fight, though."

WILSON RANCH

The sun was settling into the horizon as Flynn rode up to the front of the white picket fence with Newton alongside.

Lucy was standing inside the fence, with her arms folded across her chest, her dog Garin sat beside he, but got to his feet as he and Newton spied each other.

"About time, Uncle Mason," she said, matter of factly.

"Lucy, you better come here and give me a hug," he said as he stepped down from the outlaw's grulla gelding.

He caught her and returned the hug as she jumped up and threw her arms about his neck. "I'm so sorry about Laddie, Uncle Mason."

He set her down and looked at her. "Thank you…But, how did you…Oh, never mind."

"I could feel your sorrow when you got about ten miles from here."

"Thank you, Lucy…again." He gave her another hug.

Newton and Garin circled each other several times and exchanged sniffs, getting acquainted.

"Mason," cried his sister as she came down the steps. "Fiona said you'd be here, just wasn't sure when." She came through the gate and hugged him. "I expect you're hungry."

"I could eat, Sis. Haven't had anything since breakfast, and then it was just jerky an' a stale biscuit…Where's Cletus?"

"Turn around," she replied.

He turned to see his brother-in-law striding from the barn with a pail of milk. "Well, it's a good thing, Cletus, I was hoping for a glass of fresh milk."

"Can't get any fresher'n this, Mason," he said as he handed the bucket to his wife, Mary Lou.

"Come on in, fried up a couple of pullets just for you and made one of your favorites for desert."

"That would be a apple pie with a dollop of butter on top, I would wager."

"No bet," she said as she turned and headed toward the house. "Let me put this milk in the cooling room under the house…You want sweet milk or buttermilk?"

"You got some buttermilk...I shore admire havin' about a mason jar full...You don't mind?"

"Have all you want. I know that's what Lucy likes."

The diminutive alien grinned big. "I do indeed Momma, we don't have buttermilk on my world...In fact we don't have cows."

"But you have meat," said Flynn.

"Yes, but we grow it in special factories. It has all the protein and nutrition of your beef."

"Taste the same?" he asked.

She shook her head, flipping her pixie hair about. "Not even close...Don't have pecan pie, either."

"My Lord, how do ya'll survive without buttermilk, beef, fried chicken, or pecan pie?" said Mary Lou over her shoulder as she went through the gingerbread screen door back into the house.

"I never had Terran food until we crashed...It's one of the wonderful things I truly enjoy about your world...besides my new family, of course," answered Lucy with a smile.

"Well, that was outstandin', Sis," said Mason as he pushed back from the table after they had finished off the chicken, the other dishes, and the pie.

"Actually Lucy made the pie...We've been having some lessons."

"Dang, Lucy, you did good. Couldn't tell the difference between Mary Lou's and yours," Flynn commented.

"She's a quick learner," said Mary Lou.

Mason grinned. "I would imagine...Did Fiona have anymore information on the case with Bass?"

She glanced at their adopted alien. "No, but Lucy did recommend to Bone and Loraine that they should talk to Doctor Ashalatubbi about the Indian portal thing."

"If anyone knows...*Anompoli Lawa* does," commented Flynn. "Actually, I'm kinda enjoyin' havin' them around...Hadn't been for that big lug, I would have lost my Fiona...an' our little one."

"That could be why Bone and Loraine are here...I so look forward to meeting the venerable Shaman," said Lucy as she carried the coffee pot to the table.

"Betcha we can arrange that," replied Flynn. He paused in thought. "Lucy, why don't you come with me to Gainesville? You can stay at Faye's while I go on over to Paris an' join up with Fiona an' Bass...When we're done, we can arrange the meetin' an' you'll already be there...What say?"

She smiled and nodded. "I think that would be quite appropriate." Lucy glanced at Cletus and Mary Lou.

"Don't look at us, you already know what needs to happen," said Mary Lou.

"You can ride that dun mare I've been workin' on, Lucy. She's gentle enough," added Cletus.

Flynn held his cup out to Lucy and nodded in agreement. "Just barely run it over."

She looked at him and grinned. "It's a good thing I know what you're thinking."

He winked at her, picked up his cup, blew across the top, licked the rim to cool it and took a sip. "Umm, good coffee."

"Might we leave at first light?" asked Lucy.

"My thoughts exactly," answered Flynn.

"I know." Lucy winked back and took a sip of her own coffee.

§§§

CHAPTER TWELVE

SANTA FE DEPOT
GAINESVILLE, TEXAS

"Dang, I hope we get those buckskins when we get to Paris. Gettin' a bit tired of wearing these Farmer Brown overalls," said Bone as he, Loraine, Bodie and Fiona boarded the east bound train.

"I don't know, Bone...hat looks nice, though," commented Bodie.

"Is a bit strange looking," added Loraine. "Bib overalls, a John Bull hat and your 500 strapped around your hips."

"Leastwise, I have a hat," answered Bone as he glanced at his partner.

"You know I hate hats."

"Whatever suits you," replied, Bone. "Might make you look taller, though, Pard. You need all the help you can get."

"Damn you, Bone, you just wait," Loraine responded.

"You sure ya'll ain't married?" asked Bodie.

"Oh, God," muttered Loraine.

"It's how they communicate, Bodie," said Fiona.

"Annabel would have peeled my noggin' by now, I said stuff like that," he replied as they walked down the asileway.

They picked facing double seats at the end of the passenger car and stowed their saddlebags and long guns in the open overhead rack.

"Will the horses be all right in the livestock car, since we didn't remove their saddles?" asked Loraine.

"Shore, they'll be fine. We'll be in Paris before noon...Only have a stop in Dennison. They got water, plus they're all good trail horses…used to wearin' their tack…long as the cinches ain't too tight."

"Is that why we loosened them before the hostler led them up the ramp?" she inquired.

"Dang, Pard, you're quick," quipped Bone sitting beside her.

He and Loraine had picked the backward facing seats while Bodie and Fiona sat in the forward ones.

"Keep it up, Bone, just keep it up…Remember the hot coals?" Loraine replied.

"Oh, yeah…I'll be sure to put my bedroll on the other side of camp."

"Won't save you," she retorted.

The car lurched as the big black 4x4x2 coal-fired locomotive chugged out of the station, belching clouds of black smoke and headed east.

"Accordin' to Ranger Captain Bill McDonald down to Austin…there's a train robbery in Texas every three days," said Bodie sitting across from Bone and Loraine.

"Still? In this day and time?" asked Loraine.

"What he says," Bodie answered. "He keeps track of stuff like that for the Rangers."

"God help 'em if any hoodlums try to hit this train," said Bone.

The train slowed as it made the only curve in the tracks en-route to Paris at the small community of Woodbine between Gainesville and Whitesboro.

Four men on horseback burst out of the woods on the north side of the tracks and sprinted alongside the red caboose. Gravel and crushed rock flew from their horse's pounding hooves.

Three of the riders were able to grab the iron handles on the side of the slow moving car and swung aboard the platform between it and the livestock car.

The fourth man gathered their loose mounts and reined to a walk as the train picked up speed again.

The three train robbers climbed to the top of the livestock car, ran along the center ridge to the platform of the first of two passenger cars between them and the express car.

They climbed down the ladder, gathered at the back door of the passenger car, pulled their neckerchiefs over the lower half of their faces and drew their sidearms.

"We'll hit the passengers then see what's in the express car." The leader nodded at the man nearest to the door.

He opened it, the three stepped in, and moved about a third of the way down the aisleway.

The robber in the rear turned and faced the passengers at the back of the car while the other two faced the front.

"Awright, pilgrims, this is a holdup. Do what we say an' nobody gits hurt…Don't nobody be stupid now," said the man in the front.

"Now, fellers," said Bodie from the back seat facing the third outlaw. "You're tryin' to rob a train with a Texas Ranger an' a Deputy US Marshal ridin' on it."

He pointed at the badge pinned to his gray wool vest, and then at Fiona's on her bustier. "Ain't the smartest thing I ever heard of."

"Guess you ain't noticed, lawdog, we got the guns and mine's pointed at you," said the robber. "Now, let's have yer wallets and watches."

He glanced down at Bone facing the opposite direction. "You too, farmer...an' gimmie that hat, too."

"Aw, please, mister, this was a gift from my mama...God rest her soul," said Bone as he twisted around.

"Don't care 'bout yer life story, bumkin, jest gimmie the hat an' yer money."

"Yessir...Jest please don't hurt me...Got six kid to feed."

The robber failed to notice the slight smirk on Fiona's face.

The other two had moved up the aisleway holding out small flour sacks to the rest of the passengers collecting their valuables.

Bone appeared to reach for his wallet, but came out with his .50 cal, quickly rose to his full 6'8" height like a giant cat, and shoved the monstrous barrel against the unsuspecting man's forehead, thumbing the hammer back ominously at the same time.

The would-be robber's eyes crossed as he tried to focus on the largest handgun in the world pressed between his eyes.

"How about I just scatter your brains all the way to the front of the car?" Bone hissed as he grabbed the man's Colt in his massive left hand and twisted it from his grip, breaking his index finger in the process.

"Ow, ow, ow…my fanger!"

To Bone's side and behind him, Loraine, Bodie and Fiona had gotten to their feet with guns drawn and pointed at the other two outlaws.

"Now you two malefactors drop those weapons, right now, and you might live to see another sunrise," said Fiona as she cocked both of her .38-40 Peacemakers.

The two astonished robbers up the aisleway spun around.

"Clel, you stupid bastard, how'd that big hayseed git the jump on you?" said the leader from the front as he grabbed the woman passenger on his left and jerked her to her feet.

"Let her go," said an unemotional Fiona.

"Guess not…Meby I'll jest punch a hole in this little lady." His thumb pulled the hammer back. "Now ya'll…"

There was a huge roar inside the confined passenger car, followed by a giant white cloud of acrid gunsmoke and a woman's piercing scream.

As the smoke began to dissipate out the numerous open windows along the sides of the car, it was obvious that both the outlaw and the woman were crumpled in a heap in the middle of the aisleway.

The third robber dropped his Colt to the floor and held both hands over his head—there was a yellow puddle gathering around his feet.

"I give...I give," he screamed.

Bone popped the robber in front of him across the top of his head with the barrel of his hand cannon, sending him instantly to the floor like a bag of wet grain.

The forward door of the car burst open and the blue-clad conductor rushed in holding a Webley Bulldog in his hand. "What the Sam Hill's goin' on here?"

"These idiots tried to rob a train with a Texas Ranger, a Deputy US Marshal and two police officers as passengers," said Fiona as she returned her Colts to her cross-draw holsters under her morning coat.

BONE

"My Lord in Heaven." The conductor knelt beside the woman passenger lying in the aisleway.

"Is she…" one of the other passengers started to ask.

"Don't look like it," he said as he patted her hand. "Think she just fainted."

The woman stirred, put her hand to her head and asked, "What happened?"

She glanced at the outlaw lying next to her and saw the two pencil-sized holes in his forehead less than a quarter of an inch apart. Blood was slowly weeping from the holes and pooling on the worn carpet in the aisleway. She fainted again.

Bodie glanced out the window on his side of the car to see the fourth would-be robber galloping alongside with the other three horses in tow.

The outlaw noticed the gunsmoke blowing out of the windows from the moving train. He dropped the reins of the other mounts and spurred his horse back into the woods that bordered the tracks on both sides.

"Huh, the horse holder got cold feet looks like," he said. "I'll send a telegram back to Sheriff Durbin in Gainesville when we hit Dennison…Shouldn't be too hard to fine that nabob with the description I'll give him," said Ranger Hickman.

"Looks like robbers aren't any brighter in this day and time as they are in ours," Bone whispered. "We had a real num-nuts one time that tried to hold up a liquor store with a toy gun. Didn't know the owner was an inactive Marine...Like to have beat him to death with a baseball bat before my Pard and I could pull him off." He grinned at Loraine.

"Do you think he learned a lesson?" asked Fiona.

"Probably not, replied Loraine with a grin.

"What's a liquor store?" asked Bodie.

Bone looked at him with a puzzled expression. "It's a store like any other, except they only sell liquor, wine and beer."

"You're joshin'?" exclaimed Bodie.

"Kid you not," replied Bone.

"Dang, what'll they think of next?" muttered Bodie.

Bone and Loraine both had big grins on their faces.

"You wouldn't believe, Ranger...literally," said Bone.

"You say so…Let's get these miscreants an' the body moved back into the caboose," said Bodie.

"Good idea," said Fiona.

She looked at the two remaining outlaws. The one Bone hit over the head was starting to come to. He shook his head and sat up with a confused look on his face.

"Where am I?" he asked.

"In deep trouble, slick," said Bodie.

"You two, grab your friend, follow me…Bodie, loan me your shackles, I only have one."

Fiona led the way out the back, across the two platforms and into the caboose. The two dejected men followed, carrying the body between them.

Fiona returned a few minutes later and took her seat next to Bodie.

"How did you know he wouldn't shoot that woman?" asked Bodie.

She smiled. "I wasn't about to give him the opportunity…Not a time for negotiation…"

Bone nodded. "It was a time for action…To quote the Greek philosopher, Heraclitus, 'change is the only constant in life'…I like to add…except for human nature."

Loraine gave him a surprised look. "Bone, I would have never expected you to quote something so academic."

He shrugged. "Got it from my granma."

§§§

CHAPTER THIRTEEN

**KATY DEPOT
PARIS, TEXAS**

The big black locomotive blew huge clouds of steam from her boilers to relieve the working pressure when she rolled to a stop next to the red brick platform.

Fiona and the others grabbed their saddlebags and long guns from the overhead rack and made their way to the exit at the front of the car.

Bone was the last to step down from the iron steps to the ground. He looked around as the other passengers disembarked and met acquaintances or family.

"Anybody see Bass?" he asked.

"Nobody sees Bass Reeves until he wants you to," said Fiona.

A gray-haired slumped-shouldered black porter in a white hip-length jacket and a short-billed, flat-topped blue railroad hat rolled a luggage cart up to the group.

"Ya'll good folks got'ny luggage you want's me to put on my cart here?"

"Just what we're carryin'...Is there a good hotel you can recommend with a livery nearby?" asked Bodie.

"Yassuh, yassuh, sho is." The colored man pointed down the street. "The Red River Ho-tel two blocks thataway with they own livery next door...It's right clean an' gots a good eatin' place downstairs, too."

Bodie slipped the porter two-bits. "Thank you."

"Yassuh, thank you, suh." He slipped the coin in his pocket and moved on off to some other passengers.

Bodie turned back to the others. "Well, shall we get our mounts and head down that way…We can go downstairs after we check in an' get some lunch."

"You and Marshal Selden Lindsey's partner, Marshal Hart up at Ardmore, always thinking about eating," said Fiona with a grin.

"I'm a growin' boy…'sides it'll make it easy for Bass to find us," retorted Bodie.

Fiona smiled again. "That won't be necessary."

"Why not?" asked Bone.

"He already found us…Bodie gave him a quarter…Don't look," commented Fiona.

"That was…" Loraine started.

"It was," said Fiona as the porter disappeared inside the depot with a cart full of luggage. "I worked with him for two years. He loves undercover disguises…Even his own son didn't recognize him one time."

"Was that his son, Bennie?"

Fiona nodded at Bone.

"That when he had to arrest him for killing his wife?" asked Bone.

"He arrested his own son?" inquired an astonished Loraine.

"He did. To Bass, the law isn't everything…it's the only thing…He said that since Bennie was his son, it was up to him to arrest him…He was afraid another marshal might shoot Bennie…or get shot. He never shirked what he considered his responsibility."

"From what I've read, he was…uh, is the epitome of a real lawman," said Loraine.

"He is that. The newspapers call him the indomitable marshal," added Fiona.

"That was the great Bass Reeves…Dang, who knew?"

"That's the point, Bone," said Fiona.

RED RIVER HOTEL

The four law officers trotted up to the Red River Livery next to the hotel and dismounted.

A smallish Indian man stepped out of the big double open doorway to the stable.

"How do, I am called *Hushi Ushta*…that Choctaw for Four Sparrows. Most call me *Hushi* or just Injun."

"Why Four Sparrows?" asked Bodie.

"Take four to make mess. Me not very big...You want stable horses an'..." He glanced at Fiona's mule, Spot. "...an' spirit mule."

"Spirit mule?" asked Fiona. "How do you mean?"

"Painted mule revered by Choctaw...Blessed by *Chí-hóo-wah*, the Great Spirit."

"I can understand that," said Fiona. "Yes, please and give them all an extra bait of grain. We should be leaving tomorrow."

She looked at the corral next to the big barn. "Nice looking gray Saddlebred stallion."

"Uhh, belong big man of color. Him know Choctaw language."

"What's his name?" asked Bone.

"No say."

"You mean he didn't tell you his name?" inquired Loraine.

"No...Him say no say," answered *Hushi*.

Fiona leaned over to Bone. "He means he was told not to give out his name...But, that's Flash, Bass' horse."

"Oh, right...Makes sense."

"What do we owe for each animal?" asked Fiona.

"You stay hotel?" asked *Hushi*.

"Yes," she replied.

"Pay less. Fifty cents per day plus 25 cents for extra grain. *Hushi* brush, check feet. Replace shoe if need...no charge...Spirit Mule no charge. It honor for *Hushi* care for."

Fiona smiled and nodded at the Choctaw. "*Chí-hóo-wah-bia-chi.*"

Hushi beamed at her as they walked toward the front door of the hotel.

"What was that you said?" asked Loraine.

"Go with God," replied Fiona.

"*Chí-hóo-wah* means God?" asked Bone. "It sounds almost like..."

"Jehovah...I know," answered Fiona as they went through the door into the lobby of the hotel. "The Muskogean group of Indian tribes of the southeast's word *Chí-hóo-wah*, means God or the Great Spirit and has been used for several thousand years."

"You mean..."

Fiona interrupted Loraine again. "There is apparently some connection between the Jews of ancient Israel, the Hebrew language and the Amerindians of the southeast."

"Ever hear of the lost tribe of Israel, Pard?" asked Bone.

"Of course…So you're saying they wound up in North America before the birth of Christ?"

"What do you think?" he asked.

"Stunned, is what I think. This changes everything we thought we knew about our history."

"Yeah…So much for Columbus," added Bone.

"May I help you?" asked the slightly built balding clerk behind the counter.

"I'm Deputy US Marshal Fiona Flynn. We need…"

"Yes, Marshal Flynn, I already have you booked for two rooms." He turned the large register book around. "Just sign in, please," he said.

"I'll probably need another room for me when my husband joins us. I just don't know exactly when he will be here."

"Yes, Ma'am. I'll hold a room available."

"Thank you…and don't call me Ma'am…Marshal will be fine." Her steel-gray eyes snapped at him.

"Uh, yes…Uh, Marshal." He laid two keys on the counter.

"Do the rooms have two beds?" asked Bone.

"Yes, sir."

"It's a good thing. Don't think me and the Ranger here could fit on one."

The clerk looked the two men up and down. "No, sir."

He looked at the register after the four of them had signed.

"Mister Bone and Miss Rodriguez?"

They both turned toward the clerk.

"I have some packages for you." He reached under the counter and pulled out two large bundles and set them on top.

"Ha, the buckskins I betcha," said Bone. "Thank the Lord." He handed the smaller of the two bundles to Loraine and tucked the other under his arm. "Figure the little one is yours, Pard."

She grinned at him. "You think?…I'm amazed they could find enough deer to make yours to get them here in time…Not counting the time to make them. Can't believe the Cherokee ladies could make them this quick."

"My grandmother has a group of about twenty or so Cherokee women who make leather clothing commercially," commented Fiona. "They can turn most things out overnight."

BONE

"We need to send them some money for these," said Loraine.

"They only accept money for the Cherokee orphan school," replied Fiona.

"Let's send 'em five hundred dollars…What do you think, Pard?" said Bone.

"At least," she replied.

Bone and Bodie headed for the stairs.

"Hill Country Leather Goods must have had a sale."

"Who?" asked Bodie.

"Never mind," Bone replied with a grin.

SKEANS BOARDING HOUSE

Flynn and Lucy opened the gingerbread screen door to the boarding house, stepped inside, followed by Newton, and turned left into the parlor. The day was pleasant and the main door was standing open allowing the stately Victorian house to breathe.

"Faye! Are you in the kitchen?" his voice was only slightly above normal.

"Mason! Ya'll are already here. Fiona didn't know how long it would take you to track down that outlaw," Faye said as she came through the swinging door from the kitchen.

She stepped over, gave him a hug and then looked down. "And you must be Lucy...So pleased to have you in my home." Faye held out her hand.

"It's wonderful to meet you, Miz Skeans."

"Oh, fiddle-de-dee, call me Faye. I feel like I already know you from what Fiona and Mason have told me...and look, here's Newton, too." She reached down and rubbed the top of the dog's head.

"Where are Bodie and Annabel?" asked Flynn.

"Bodie went with Fiona and them and Annabel took the twins out to Frances Ann's for a visit with her and her little one.

Faye glanced over her shoulder back at the white swinging door into the kitchen on the other side of the dining room. "But you'll never guess who else is here."

"I've been so looking forward to meeting *Anompoli Lawa*," said Lucy.

"But, how did...Oh, of course. I forgot. I understand you know what people around you are going to say before they say it...Doctor Ashalatubbi, someone here to meet you."

BONE

The sixty year old, white-haired Shaman, medical doctor and spiritual leader of the Chickasaw tribe came through the door holding a white mug. "Sorry, I was refilling my coffee cup."

He looked at Lucy, sat his cup on an end table beside a green velvet Chippendale fainting couch and stepped forward to the diminutive alien. "*Shee-ah*, it is a pleasure, great Sky Queen, I am at your service." He tilted his head toward her and held out his hand.

Lucy blushed and took the Shaman's hand and held it in both of hers.

The two stood silently staring at each other's eyes—neither moved or blinked.

Faye and Flynn nervously exchanged glances.

"Would ya'll like to have a seat?" she asked.

There was no response or movement from Lucy or Doctor Ashalatubbi.

Finally they broke their reverie and looked at both Faye and Mason.

"I apologize," said Lucy. "We were exchanging information.

"Oh, of course…I knew that," said Flynn.

"She reinforced many of my beliefs, filled in some gaps and taught me a number of things I wasn't aware of...I am humbled," the Shaman said.

Lucy looked at him. "And you taught me things I wasn't aware of with the long history of your people and mine, also, *Anompoli Lawa*."

"In just those few moments?" asked Faye.

Lucy and Winchester exchanged glances again and both smiled.

"We covered many thousands of years of our history with the sky beings...We opened our minds to each other," said the Shaman.

"We finally convinced the Chickasaw and other tribes in the Americas to stop referring to the *Anunnaki* as gods...but as teachers instead," added Lucy.

"Where did the name *Anunnaki*, come from?" asked Faye.

"The ancient Sumerians...It's their word meaning, *Those who from the Heavens came*," said Lucy.

"But what does that have to do with how Bone and Loraine got here?" inquired Flynn.

"Lucy and I know they came through an ancient portal in Palo Pinto County." *Anompoli Lawa* glanced at her. "The gates or portals throughout the world were placed here by a different group of the *Anunnaki* than Lucy's people…The most widely known is at Tiahuanaco, in Bolivia…known as The Gate Of The Sun."

"Just so you know, there are several thousand races throughout our galaxy, most of them humanoid…We are but one. Many, however, do not possess space travel, yet…like you Terrans…but several have the ability to create recurring electromagnetic vortexes which can fold time and space and act as portals in the space/time continuum…We just don't know exactly how they are activated," said Lucy.

"But my people do," said *Anompoli Lawa.*

§§§

CHAPTER FOURTEEN

RED RIVER HOTEL
PARIS, TEXAS

"Dang! These things fit like a glove," said Bone as he looked in the mirror above the sideboard at his new buckskins. "Can't believe how soft they are."

"You mean like they were made for you?...Sonofagun, who knew?" quipped Bodie with a slight grin.

"Smart ass," commented Bone. "Huh, what's this? A purse?" He picked up a beaded bag about ten inches square, with a long strap attached, from his bed. "Must be for Loraine."

"Nope. 'Magine she's got one too...Indians call it a parfleche. It's an old French word meaning bag...Woodsmen refer to it as a 'possibles' bag. Keep stuff like flint and steel or waxed matches, some jerky, fishin' line, hooks, foldin' knife...stuff that you might need out in the woods," informed Bodie. "You wear it strapped across your chest."

"Hellova idea. So cool."

"So, never met Bass, huh?" asked Bodie.

"Nope, just read a lot about him...The US Marshals Service is building a museum in Fort Smith. They put a larger than life statue of Bass on his horse, Flash, out in front. Consider him the greatest marshal in their history."

"Why doesn't that surprise me...I've known Bass a number of years...worked with him a whole bunch of times, an' never known him to show the slightest bit of excitement under any circumstance...Don't think the man knows what fear is."

"Kind of what I read…Always dreamed of how it would be to live back in this time…Felt like I was born about a hundred and fifty years too late."

"What did you read? Penny dreadfuls and such?"

"Oh, no, westerns were really big back or I guess I should say up in my time. There's going to be a whole load of writers to write full blown quality novels about this part of the history of the US…They'll call them 'Westerns'."

"Really? You mean writers like Jules Verne, Jane Austen and Mark Twain?"

"Oh, yeah, a bunch of 'em. Guys like Louis L'Amour, Zane Grey, Ken Farmer, Brad Dennison, Lou Bradshaw and Larry McMurtry, among others…That McMurtry fellow even wins a Pulitzer Prize for a book called *Lonesome Dove* about a cattle drive from Texas to the Montana territory…It's the highest award there is in literature," said Bone.

"You got to be joshin'."

"Kid you not, Ranger…Let's go check on Loraine and see how her getup fits."

They stepped across the hall and rapped on the door. Loraine opened it also wearing her buckskins and moccasins.

"How do you like 'em, Pard?"

"OMG, Bone, they're like wearing pajamas, but fit better...everywhere. They're unbelievably soft," she said as he and Bodie entered. "I love the beaded purse they included."

"I got one too...But it's called a parfleche," said Bone.

"How do you know that?"

He glanced at Bodie and grinned. "Magic."

"Told you how comfortable they were," commented Fiona. "I won't wear anything else when I have to go tracking into the woods...or anywhere else. They're virtually impervious to tearing, many times better than canvas for protecting your skin...and if you get wet, they dry just as soft as they were originally...It's called brain cured." She looked at Loraine and cocked an eyebrow. "OMG?"

"Short for, 'Oh, my God'. Just something we say back home. We abbreviate a lot of things...Brain cured?" asked Loraine.

"They rub crushed deer brain into the leather as part of the tanning process...Makes it super soft."

"Wow," Loraine replied as she closed the door behind Bone and Bodie. "What are the soles? They seem thicker."

"They use elk rump hide when they can. If that's not available they use skin from the hump or neck of a bull…It's tougher, but still quiet and protect your feet when going over rocky ground," said Fiona. "I think ya'll are going to love them."

"I already…"

Loraine was interrupted by a knock on the door. She turned back around and opened it.

A large, broad-shouldered black man in a black three piece suit and a Prince of the Plains Stetson stood in the hall along with shorter slight-built younger man also in a suit and a bowler. They both quickly removed their hats as she stepped back.

"Kin we come in?" He glanced up and down the hall both ways.

"Bass…Ya'll come on in," said Fiona from behind Loraine.

The two men came inside and Fiona quickly stepped over and hugged the big man's neck.

"So good to see you, Bass."

"Good to see you, too, Fiona." He quickly took in the entire room. "Bodie." He nodded at the ranger, frowned at Bone and Loraine and looked back at Fiona.

"Bass, this is Dectective Bone and Inspector Loraine Rodriquez...Just call them Bone and Loraine. They're cops."

"Uh, huh...Ain't many men I gots to look up to to go eye to eye...Looks like you could go bear huntin' with a switch." Bass grinned. "Had to go knuckles an' skulls with a little feller like you once...Named Bear Man Bannack...Don't think I'd much want to do it again."

Bone grinned at the marshal.

Bass paused and pointed to the smaller man with him. "This here's Secret Service agent Wesley Thomas."

Fiona glanced at the agent. "I think ya'll should have a seat on the bed over there...This may take a while...Then you can fill us in on this operation."

Bass raised his eyebrows and looked at Thomas as they sat down on one of the beds. "'Spect this is gonna be good, Wesley...When Fiona Mae tells you to sit down to tell you somethin', count on it bein' a real doozie."

Bone, Loraine and Bodie took a seat on the other bed while Fiona straddled the only chair in the room backwards and leaned her elbows on the back.

Thirty minutes later she finished as Bass and Wesley exchanged glances, and then looked at Bone and Loraine with wide eyes.

Bass leaned over to Wesley and whispered, "See, tol' you."

"Well, there you have it. Now, whether you believe it or not, is up to you…But, it is what it is," Fiona said. "To quote Shakespeare, 'Time travels at different speeds for different people. I can tell you who time strolls for, who it trots for, who it gallops for, and who it stops cold for'."

Bass shook his head. "Well, if that don't put the rag on the bush, or as Jack would say, 'Slap Aunt Gussie in the face an' double rectify me'."

"We don't really understand it either, Bass, but, we're here and I suppose we'll stay till we or possibly Doctor Ashalatubbi and Lucy can figure out how to get us home…after figuring out why we're here in the first place," said Bone.

"I've already seen them in action, Bass. They can be right handy. Like I mentioned, he saved my life and their firearms are something else…Now why did you ask me here?…Oh, and Mason will be joining us."

Bass looked at the Secret Service agent. "Well, reckon this may work out after all…Mason is her husband. Tol' you 'bout him…I'll, uh…let Wesley here, 'splain to ya'll what we think is 'bout to come down.

Another thirty minutes went by before the agent finished debriefing Fiona and the others.

"You mean Teddy Roosevelt is right here in this hotel, agent Thomas?" asked Bone.

"On the floor above us…along with his retinue."

Bass looked at Wesley with a puzzled expression. "His what?"

"Entourage…assistants."

"Oh…lackeys." Bass nodded. "They's five of 'em altogether."

"Hope they don't get in the way," said Fiona.

"It's possible, but our main responsibility is the Assistant Secretary," said Thomas.

Bone and Loraine exchanged glances.

"Yeah, you wouldn't believe," muttered Bone.

"How do you mean, Bone?" asked the agent.

"Well, don't guess it will hurt to tell ya'll since you already know we're from the future." Bone took a deep breath and looked at Loraine. "Theodore Roosevelt will become the 26th President of the United States in 1901...in our timeline, and that could be that's why we're here."

He looked at Loraine again, and then back at Bass and Wesley. "Unless we fail and then all of our history will change."

"Great guns," exclaimed Wesley, and then he continued, "Like I said, Spain hates him with a passion because he's made no secret he wants them out of Cuba...One way or another," said Wesley.

"Yep...He's sending the United States newest battleship *USS Maine* to Havana...It's going to blow up and sink in the harbor on February 18, 1898, in just a few months...The US is going to blame Spain and the Spanish American War will start in April," said Bone.

"Lawdy, Lawdy," commented Bass as he got to his feet and paced across the room.

"Teddy will resign as Assistant Secretary of the Navy, enlist in the Army and form a company called the Rough Riders to fight in Cuba under his leadership," added Bone. "I study American history."

He shrugged. "The war will only last four months...Teddy Roosevelt will be termed a hero."

"So, we have to make sure he survives his hunting trip to the Seven Devil hills in the Kiamichis," said Fiona.

"Pretty much," replied Bone.

"What happens on this trip?" asked Wesley.

Bone shook his head. "No clue. There's no mention of this particular trip in the history books."

"Sounds like we go with the flow," said Loraine.

"How did ya'll find out about this kidnappin'," asked Bodie.

"Somehow, Spain found out he was coming down here to hunt bear, panther, and wolves in the Kiamichis," Thomas paused and nodded to Bass.

"I had paper on three ne'er-do-wells fer larceny of horses...Catched 'em an' made 'em walk twenty miles back to town without they boots." Bass chuckled. "Time we gots there they was singin' all sorts of tunes, includin' that they was on the way here to Paris as hired gunhawks to help kidnap some government big wig fer a Spaniard."

Bass took out his battered old rosewood pipe, filled it and lit it with a match from his vest pocket. He took a couple of puffs and exhaled an aromatic light blue cloud over his head.

"I passes the information up the line...Marshal Taylor, up to the Washington City office, gots a special deputy marshal an' two other marshals to work they way in to replace them three I arrested an' infiltrate the bunch...undercover."

Thomas took over. "The Office of the United States Marshal contacted the Secret Service because it involved part of the administration and we were already investigating a counterfeiting ring here in northeast Texas...So we put the pieces together and here we are."

"Who are the other three marshals," asked Fiona.

Bass grinned. "Aw, jest some old hard cases...Selden Lindsey, Jack McGann and Brushy Bill Roberts."

"Holy cow!" Bone shot to his feet.

"Oh, my, my, my. Those three and us...What a hand to draw to," said Fiona with a smile that extended across her face.

BONE

"I'd say," replied Bass as he blew a maple flavored smoke ring over his head and watched it slowly float up to the twelve foot embossed tin ceiling.

§§§

CHAPTER FIFTEEN

RED RIVER HOTEL
PARIS, TEXAS

"When do we leave, Mister Roosevelt?" asked the gun bearer, Marvin Wilhite.

"Telegram I received said we should wait until tomorrow. We'll be contacted by my escort from the Secret Service...a Wesley Thomas."

"Don't understand why it's necessary to have a Secret Service agent along for," commented Wilhite.

"Politics, my boy...damned politics," said Teddy as he lit a Virginia cigar and paced the room.

He walked past the open door of the suite that led to the adjoining room. The four other men in Roosevelt's group were inside, playing poker, killing time.

"Bossman's a bit restless...Call," commented his assistant Reginald Baker after glancing into the other room.

There was a knock at the door of Loraine and Fiona's room. Loraine opened it to see Mason, Lucy and Doctor Ashalatubbi standing out in the hall with Newton sitting beside them.

"Mason!" said Fiona as she rushed to her husband and pulled him in the room, covering his face with kisses.

Lucy and the doctor stood in the doorway, grinning at Flynn and his wife.

Fiona finally broke from their embrace and noticed the small childlike woman and the venerable Shaman. "Lucy, Winchester...come in, come in. You too, Newton."

Loraine moved back with a big smile on her face and hugged Lucy after she stepped into the room. "I didn't know you were coming."

"*Anompoli Lawa* and I didn't give Mason much of a choice," said Lucy.

"*Shee-ah, Anompoli Lawa*," greeted Bass.

"*Shee-ah, Kowishto' Losa'*...Bass Reeves," answered Doctor Ashalatubbi as he grasped the marshal's hand and forearm with both of his hands.

"Is that Chickasaw?" asked Bone.

"Yes, answered the doctor, *Shee-ah* is a greeting and he called me by my tribal name, *Anompoli Lawa,* which means He Who Talks to Many and I referred to him with his Chickasaw name, *Kowishto' Losa'*, that means Big Black Cougar." He looked up at the big man. "You would have to be Bone, I take it?"

"Yes, sir, and this is my partner, Loraine."

After all the greetings were finished, Fiona introduced Lucy to Bass and the Secret Service agent and then introduced Mason to Wesley.

"Finally I gets to meet the great Sky Queen." Bass tilted his head and softly took her tiny hand in his. Immediately he had a montage of quick flashing images *a—triangle shaped silver spacecraft—a lavender sky with two suns—a space battle with large triangle ships, small triangle fighters and giant green globes—two small gray people in hooded suits with large almond-shaped black eyes, in a type of cockpit—a windmill coming fast in the cockpit window—a flash of light.* He quivered slightly and released her hand.

"Are you all right, Bass?" asked Fiona.

He nodded. "Jest seen some things when we touched is all."

"Oh, yes, I'm familiar with that," Fiona commented.

"Just call me Lucy, Bass. I've heard so much about you…and like Fiona, Mason and Bone, you are a sender-receiver."

"Feared I don't know what that is, Lucy."

"It means your mind is open to mine."

He blinked several times. "Uh, huh…That's what it was awright." He turned to the agent. "This here's a agent from our government's Secret Service…Wesley Thomas."

"How do you do, Miss." He took her hand but didn't get any images.

"Wesley, if'n you thought Bone and Loraine's story was unusual, this'un here's goin' to be another layer on that cake."

"How so, Bass?" he asked.

Newton padded over and licked Lucy's hand. She leaned down and rubbed his head. "Good to see you, too, Newton."

Bone stepped in to explain, "You see, Lucy is a survivor of that space ship that crashed at Aurora, Texas in April of 1897...She's...well...she's from another world."

"Great guns," Wesley exclaimed almost staggering. "I guess this is my day for new things to learn."

"We're not much different from your race, Mister Thomas...just a little smaller," said Lucy.

"Among a few other things," added Fiona with a grin.

Wesley shook his head and had a wry smile. "As Marshal Flynn said earlier, 'It is what it is.' I suppose that since everyone is here, I should go upstairs to Mister Roosevelt's room and inform him we can leave in the morning for the Seven Devil Hills."

BONE

After Thomas left the room, Bass glanced at Bone's .50 cal on his hip. "Mind if'n I takes a gander at that big shooter you got there, Bone...Like to see Loraine's too."

Bone shucked the five rounds from his 500 and handed it to Bass.

"Good goshamighty," Bass exclaimed. "This is a dang cannon...Good balance though."

"Fellows in my time have been known to hunt grizzlies armed only with this weapon...It's the most powerful handgun in the world," said Bone.

"I kin believe that." He handed it back to Bone who reloaded it and dropped it back into his new holster.

Loraine popped the magazine from her Kimber and handed it to Bass. "This is a semiautomatic .45 caliber with an eight round capacity magazine...Will fire as fast as you can pull the trigger."

"Dadgum...'Course only takes one, if'n it's placed right," said Bass.

Loraine grinned. "True, but it's kind of handy when you're faced with three or four bad guys."

"Well, gotta agree with that, little lady." He handed it back. She slipped the magazine in the grip and slapped the bottom to make sure it was seated.

"Loraine can shoot the flies off a bull's butt at thirty yards, too, Bass," commented Bone.

"Gotta say I'm impressed, little lady."

Fiona turned to Bass. "So, what's the plan, Marshal Reeves?"

"Well, I knows that they's 'bout fifteen or so gunhawks a waitin' some'rs 'tween the Red an' the Kiamichis...Now, Jack, Selden an' Bill is part of that bunch, so's that cuts it down to twelve...er there 'bouts."

"Are we goin' to go along with Roosevelt's group?" asked Flynn.

"Reckon not. We's gonna split up an' half of us is gonna flank Roosevelt an' his men on one side of they trail an' the rest on t'other side...Both off far 'nough so's they don't know we be there...My gut tells me they's a plant in amongst his men." Bass reached in his coat pocket and pulled out a wad of blue neckerchiefs. He handed one to everybody in the room. "Now, each of you needs to wear these 'round yer neck or head like a Apache, so's Marshals Lindsey, McGann an' Roberts knows you ain't one of the bushwhackers...They's doin' the same."

"Is Wesley going to stay with Roosevelt?" asked Bone.

Bass nodded. "My way of thinkin'."

"How are we going to split up?" asked Fiona.

"Been cogitatin' on that," he replied. "What say that I'll be in one group with Mason an' Loraine here...an' Newton."

Fiona interrupted him. "Since you don't know, Bone was a behind enemy lines special operations warrior for the United States Marine Corps...His specialty is night time and hidden work...I can vouch for that."

"That's good...Bone you takes the other group with Fiona an' Bodie...an' like yer new buckskins...Yer gonna need 'em."

"What about *Anompoli Lawa* and me?" asked Lucy.

Bass grinned. "Well, since I doubts I kin talk ya'll into stayin' here, how's 'bout ya'll come with me, Mason an' Loraine here...Jest want ya'll to stay to the back, though...How's that sound?"

Lucy and Doctor Winchester exchanged glances and nodded.

"Glad I brought my medical bag…Just in case." The doctor grinned. "Not any need in getting another horse for Lucy. We left the one she rode to Gainesville at Faye's…She can ride with me." He glanced at her with a grin. "She's not big as a nickel."

"Plus Lucy has some special healing skills of her own, don't forget," said Bone. "I speak from experience."

Lucy tugged on Bone's sleeve for him to lean over. She whispered in his ear. "There's something about the agent. I sensed a darkness about him."

Bone looked at her and nodded.

After Thomas entered the room and showed his silver five pointed star Secret Service badge and identification to Teddy Roosevelt and the others, he took a seat at the table where the men had been playing cards.

"I need to make a run to the necessary," said Reginald Baker as he got to his feet.

"Hope everything comes out all right, Reg," commented another one of Roosevelt's assistants, Frank Warren, as Baker left the room.

BONE

"Let you know, Warren…since you seem to be keeping track," he said over his shoulder.

Roosevelt turned to Warren. "Frank, go to our guide, Possum Middens' room down the hall, and let him know to make ready to leave at dawn."

Frank jumped up. "Yessir," he answered and headed out the door.

"Remind me to stay upwind of Middens on the trail. I've killed skunks that smelled better than him," said Roosevelt showing his trademark grin below his bushy mustache.

The other men in the room nodded in agreement.

GLOVES CREEK

The sun settled on the western horizon behind the tree covered hills on the southwestern edge of the Kiamichis as Tarlton Brewster rode back into camp. He dismounted, pulled the tack from his bay gelding and picketed him with the other horses.

"Awright you bunch of whinin' titty babies, we got our orders. Roosevelt an' his bunch are headin' this way at first light." Brewster squatted next to the fire and filled his tin coffee cup.

Ken Farmer

He continued as he got back to his feet, "Check yer weapons an' ammo, an' then we'll go over the assignments. Mind it'll take 'em to mid-afternoon day after tomorra to git to that pass 'tween those first two ridges leadin' into the Seven Devils."

RED RIVER HOTEL

"We'll leave the hotel in ones an twos an' scatter out to the four cafes we gots located fer supper…Don't want to call no 'tention to ourselves," Bass said to the others. "Fiona…Know you, me an' Mason has buckskins like Bone an' Loraine. Reckon we oughta puts 'em on 'fore we leave the hotel…We'll look like hunters er woodsmen."

"I assume we'll do the same when we leave out in the morning," commented Fiona.

"My thinkin' on that, too. Jest as well let the huntin' party take out 'fore we starts driftin' up to the ferry boat…Figure we kin travel a lots faster'n Roosevelt an' them city boys once we gits on the trail."

Bone looked at Bass. "I take it that you and I will shadow Roosevelt's column from both sides and leave markers for the others to follow."

"You takes right, Bone…Sounds like you done this kinda thing afore," commented Bass.

"Just like doing recon in the Marines during combat," he answered.

"Recon?" asked Bass.

"Reconnoiter our objective."

"Ah…Understands. Locatin' the bushwhackers." agreed Bass. "Gots paper on the most of 'cm…alive er dead."

"It'll be up to ya'll to spot the malefactors before the hunting party gets to them," said Fiona.

"Yep, that's the way it works…" replied Bone. "…without them seeing us, too."

§§§

CHAPTER SIXTEEN

GATES CREEK FERRY

The hunting guide, Possum Middens, led his own horse plus the pack mule and was first on the ferry. He was followed by Teddy Roosevelt, his gun bearer and then the rest of his entourage. Lead assistant, Reginald Baker, came last with the fee for the operator.

BONE

A hand-painted sign supported by two poles at the side of the dock, read:

HORSE & RIDER - $1,
WAGON & TEAM - 6 BITS,
COACHES AND HEAVY WAGONS $1
CALVIN C. BURNS - PROPRIETOR

"Here you are, my good man," said Baker as he handed the portly, middle-aged ferry operator with over a weeks growth of stubble on his face, six one dollar bills.

"Thankee, thankee kindley...You fellers goin' huntin', air ye?" He spat a long stream of tobacco juice into the murky water and wiped his chin with the sleeve of his already grimy shirt.

"That we are...Bear or wolves," replied Baker.

"By the Lord Harry, that's a good thing. The bear an' wolves been playin' hob with the local livestock...But the worst is the catamounts. Seem to be quite a few up in the hills these days...One of 'em got a six year old child last month."

"That's too bad. We'll keep it in mind," said Baker as the owner pushed the flat-bottomed cable ferry out into the sluggish current of the Red River.

All the riders had dismounted for the two hundred yard trip across the waterway.

173

Burns' hired help, a strapping young colored man on the other side, turned the big windlass, slowly pulling the ferry across the border river between Texas and the Indian Nations.

Roosevelt fired up one of his cigars, hand-rolled from tobacco grown in Virginia, and stood at the edge of the barge looking east, down river. He watched the water, knowing it would meander its inexorable way to merge with the Mississippi and eventually flow into the Gulf of Mexico.

The ferry reached the Choctaw Nation on the north side of the river and bumped against the wooden ramp leading up the bank as Fiona, Bone and Bodie rode up back on the Texas side and dismounted.

Fiona and Bone were in their buckskins and Apache knee-high moccasins and Bodie was wearing tan canvas trail pants stuffed in his tall cavalry style boots, a gray wool vest and collarless, faded blue and white striped shirt.

His dark brown canvas trail coat was rolled and strapped on top of his soogan behind the cantle of his line-back dun mustang, Lakota Moon.

BONE

Possum Middens led the Roosevelt hunting party up the ramp and onto the bank.

"Did you hear what the ferry operator said about predators back on the other side, sir?" asked Baker.

"I did. Sounds bully to me. Bully indeed…We'll focus on hunting the wily panther. Can't have children being carried off and killed by a rogue beast…can we, Baker?" replied Roosevelt.

"No, sir, we can't. Thought you'd want to do that, Mister Roosevelt."

The ferry docked back on the Texas side. Burns lowered the ramp to allow Fiona, Bone and Bodie to lead their mounts aboard.

"Mornin', pard. This barge goin' to the Nations?" asked Bone.

Calvin looked confused, glanced across the river and then back at Bone. "Why, shore. Where'd you think she'd be a goin'?"

"Well, when you've been where I've been, you just never know."

"Huh?"

"I mean your cable there could snap and we might end up down in Shreveport, Louisiana or maybe even New Orleans," Bone grinned.

The grizzled proprietor spat into the river again, slapped his thigh and laughed. "Oh, haw, haw...See what you mean, big boy. That's a good 'un...Gotta 'member it."

Fiona poked Bone in the back with her finger. "Just pay the man, Bone."

"Only funning, Fiona, only funning," he said as he fished three dollars out of his beaded parfleche and handed them to Burns."

"That yore name?...Bone?"

"Has been since I can remember...I always came when my mama called it, so, have to assume that it was."

"Haw, that's 'nother good 'un," commented Burns.

"You entertain purty easy, there Mister Burns," said Bodie.

"'Spect so. Don't take much who-hit-John to put me splifficated neither, so...guess so," he replied as he pushed the ferry away from the shore.

"You just love playing with people, don't you, Bone?" asked Fiona when they were out of earshot of the Texas side.

He grinned. "You could say so...Keeps me entertained. But, I only do it with people I like...or people I'm fixing to hurt."

"That's a little like Bass."

"Oh, how so?" asked Bone.

"If you're ever in a potentially violent situation with Bass and you hear him start to sing an old Negro spiritual softly almost to himself, get ready. He's going to shoot somebody...I've seen him do that more than once."

"Keep that in mind. Good notice to his friends to duck or go to ground."

"That's why I mentioned it," Fiona replied with a smile. She glanced back at the shore. "Speak of the devil. Bass and them are right behind us."

"I know. Saw them on our back trail when we were about a half mile from the river," commented Bone.

"Very good, Bone. You're really improving on this trail procedure."

"Not really, Fiona. It's something we did in the Marine Corps, too. Person could get hurt if they don't watch in front, behind, to the sides...and within...Don't you think?"

"Good point...We'll move on off to the west side of Gates Creek and parallel to Roosevelt's trail. Looks like they're going to track along the east side to the Seven Devils...Leave a marker for Bass and them," said Fiona.

"Shouldn't be necessary, Marshal. If we see him I would guarantee he saw us. No need in leaving more tracks than absolutely required."

Fiona cocked her head at Bone. "Again, very good...Detective. Right you are...Let's go, then. That all right with you, Bodie?"

The ranger just grinned at her. "Fine with me, Marshal. I'm just watchin' an' learnin'...The way ya'll carry on you'd think you were related...Lead on."

Bone ducked his head and nudged his big blood bay gelding in behind Fiona and her painted mule, Spot.

As the ferry docked on the Choctaw Nation side, Bass led his group up the bank. Newton ran to some nearby bushes, marked his territory and started checking around for coon scat.

Bass turned to the others. "We'll take the east route toward the Seven Devils...Mind that Roo-se-velt bunch is a gonna foller the trail 'long the east side of Gates Creek."

"Where are Bone and them?" asked Loraine.

"They be on the west side, missy...We gots the huntin' party hemmed 'tween us."

GLOVES CREEK

"Snake, you take your bunch work toward the ridge an' find some hides on the northwest side of Gates Creek after she curves back to the east into the Kiamichis an' the pass...an' don't shoot till you got the first of Roosevelt's dandies in sight...Should be there by tomorra."

"Awright, ladies, you heard the man, let's mount up," answered Haywood.

"Tall Jim, you an' your men got the southeast side of the pass. Me an' Tobacca Bob will come in behind...Ya'll got it?"

"We ain't pilgrims, Brewster," commented Big Floyd Atkins, aka Marshal Selden Lindsey.

GATES CREEK

After Fiona, Bone and Bodie had moved up the trail several miles, the big man held up his hand for the group to stop.

He dismounted and handed his reins to Bodie. "Here, Ranger, wrangle him a while...Be back later. You got point."

"Where you goin'?" asked Bodie.

Bone looked at him and Fiona and winked. "Scoutin'...Roosevelt's bunch are walking their horses along that game trail over that way." He pointed to the east. "I can cover ground faster on foot than they can move their column and need to take a looksee at what's ahead of them...Five'll get you ten that Bass is doing the same thing on his side."

"I'm sure you're right, Bone," said Fiona.

"Fact is he an' I'll probably meet in the middle about a mile ahead of the hunters...Don't figure they'll be doing any hunting until they set a base camp on up the way into the Kiamichis...What I would do."

"Right again, Bone...Need a rifle?" Fiona asked.

Bone grinned and patted the .50 cal on his hip. "All I need is right here...Folks looking down the barrel of this thing think they're looking inside a cannon...Pretty dang intimidating."

"Good point, Bone," agreed Bodie, but the big man had already disappeared into the thick brush.

Bass dismounted from his light gray Standardbred stallion and handed the reins to Flynn. "Gonna see what's up ahead."

"Want to take Newton?" asked Flynn.

Bass looked over at the red and white Border Collie. "Shore. We been gittin' along fair-thee-well...Come on, Newt."

Flynn's dog padded over to Bass and looked up at the black man.

"Let's go, son...thataway."

They jogged around a bend in the game trail without a sound and vanished.

"Dang, he's like a ghost," said Flynn.

"He and Bone make a good team. Bone's specialty is covert operations," said Loraine.

"What's that?" asked Flynn.

"You don't know he's around until it's too late."

"Yep, just like Bass. He learned it from the Indians he lived with for two years or so at the end of the war of Northern Aggression."

"I think Bone was born to it, but got formal training in the Marine Corps," said Loraine as she dropped back alongside Winchester and Lucy.

"Ya'll doing all right?" she asked.

"We are indeed…Aren't we, Lucy?" Winchester said over his shoulder.

"Yes, very well, thank you, Loraine," said Lucy. "Bone has gone ahead of Fiona and Bodie just like Bass."

"How do you…Oh, never mind." Loraine looked at Winchester. "Doctor Ashalatubbi, do you think you can help Bone and I get back to our time?"

"I think so, Loraine, but first we need to find out why you're here."

"We thought we knew when he took that bullet for Fiona."

Anompoli Lawa looked up to see if Flynn was far enough ahead of them that he wouldn't hear.

"Yes, I know about that. He had to save his great grandmother…I learned that from Lucy."

"Right…I'm still not used to what ya'll do."

"But, there is still something else you and he have to do, before the time is right to return, my child."

"What could it be?…I just don't understand."

"We shall know soon enough, Loraine," said Lucy.

§§§

CHAPTER SEVENTEEN

GATES CREEK

Bone stood silently in the shadow underneath the cover of a large cedar tree as he watched Newton and Bass move quietly along a game trail that bordered the creek headed his direction.

Bass stopped, folded his arms over his chest and looked in the direction of the tree. "You kin come on out now, Bone."

The big man stepped out into the trail. "How in the Sam Hill did you know I was there, Bass?...Know you couldn't see me."

Bass laid his finger alongside his nose. "My smeller. Folks has different smells...White, coloreds, Injun, Mescan, Chinee...all gots different smells. Newt smelled you 'fore I did, but I caught you near fifty yards back up the trail."

"Why didn't Newton bark?"

"Didn't need to. Knowed who you was...Jest let me know somebody friendly was up here...an' then I smelled you."

"Huh, and I took a bath before we left Paris." Bone smelled his armpit.

"Don't matter none. Ain't talkin' 'bout body stink...Talkin' 'bout yer smell. You could do it with a little practice."

"Oh, you're talking about scent...I'll be darned...Good to know."

"Yep, we all gots our own *scent* like the animals does. The Seminoles I lived with could tell different Injuns apart...Never got that good my ownself...but I kin tell Injuns from whites an' whites from coloreds easy 'nuff."

"I assume you know this country," said Bone.

"I does...Me and Jack tracked the Trotters down up in the Seven Devils back over ten year ago." Bass looked around. "Ain't changed much."

"Where do you reckon they'll be setting up for the ambush?"

"I mind they'll be at the pass where Gates Creek drains out of the hills. The Seven Devils is on the southeast side of the creek an they's a ridge of the Kiamichi Mountains on the other...Purty wooded, 'cept down by the creek where they be occasional glens an' glades along both sides."

"How did ya'll catch the Trotters?"

"Wellsir, I went in to they camp as a wanted outlaw, Satan Shields...on the run fer killin' six men in a saloon in Denison, Texas with a ax handle."

"Dang...They bought it, I guess."

"They did, 'cept Dirty Bill Trotter an' his brother Chesley, captured Jack...Knowed he was a marshal an' wanted me to kill 'im."

"Guess that didn't work."

"Nope, I went to swing that ax handle at Jack, but, redirected at Chesley holdin' a coach gun on 'im, broke his arm, an' then back swung with a uppercut. That ax handle took most of his teeth out an' knocked him cold as a wedge."

"What about Dirty Bill?" asked Bone.

Bass chuckled. "When he was distracted with me smackin' his brother 'cross the mouth, Jack jerked the ten gauge he was a holdin' out of his hand an' poleaxed him upside his head with it...Broke his neck, it did...which wuz jest as well fer as I wuz concerned. The worthless scum an' his brother was usin' his own fifteen year old daughter, Mame, fer they own needs."

"Bastards," Bone hissed.

"I 'dopted her an' her little brother. Done already had ten, five boys and five girls...figured two more wouldn't make no matter...Didn't have the heart to turn 'em over to the state...I done been a slave, Bone, wadn't 'bout to make no innocent chile one."

"Yeah, heard that...Didn't kill the brother, Chesley?"

"Naw, he had a broke arm an' no teeth left...Knowed he was gonna git hung back in Texas when we turned him over to the Rangers, anyhoo."

"Too good for him."

"Meby, but, I wanted him to be thinkin' on it some while we hauled his sorry ass over to Antlers to rendezvous with the rangers who come up from Texas by train to git 'im."

"You say Jack and them will be wearing these blue bandanas, too?" Bone touched the kerchief he'd tied around his head like an Apache headband.

"Yep, be hard to miss, anyhoo. Selden is a big broad-shouldered feller...not big as you, but big enough...Got a bushy black mustache. Brushy Bill is only 'bout five feet seven er so an' Jack's built like a bull...He's got a full brown mustache."

"That's good to know, too."

"Be tomorrow late 'fore the hunters kin git to the pass. Figure they'll pitch camp 'bout five mile up the trail...We will too," added Bass.

"I'm going to slip up that way toward the pass and find some of those boys tonight...See if I can reduce the odds a bit," said Bone with a grin.

"Don't let 'em see you," Bass commented.

Bone held up his right wrist and showed Bass his bracelet.

"What's that?"

"A little something Lucy gave me up in our time."

BONE

Bone touched two of the turquoise stones embedded in the solid gold links. The air around him shimmered briefly and he disappeared.

Bass glanced around surprised. "Where'd you go, Bone?...I smells you, but cain't see you."

A few seconds later, the air shimmered again and Bone became visible again.

"Haints!"

"Not really, Bass, it's a device her race developed that bends the light around whoever is wearing this." He held up his arm again. "When I touch two of these stones, it activates it and no one can see me...I touch the stones again to turn it off."

"Jesus, Mary, Joseph an' all the disciples...Better'n haints...Sho'nuff come in handy sometimes."

Bone grinned again . "Like now...Going to rattle their cage some."

"Now that I thunk on it, believe I'll go with you. Fiona an' Flynn kin keep track of Roosevelt an' his bunch...Should find some of them nabobs 'round nightfall."

Bone grinned and nodded. "My favorite time."

GLOVES CREEK

Snake Smith's and Tall Jim's groups pitched camp together alongside the banks of the creek. Gloves Creek ran north and then east five miles to the south side of the Seven Devil Hills. It would merge with Gates Creek on down south toward Paris.

They had watered and picketed their horses on some good grass down close to the creek.

"Come first light, we'll head on to the pass and split up like we planned," said Smith.

"Yeah, have to go cold camp once we're in position," added Big Floyd, aka Selden Lindsey. "Jest as well have a hot supper while we got the chance."

"I could use a cup of coffee, too…Reckon where Brewster and Tobacca Bob is?"

"Back behind us som'eres, I mind…Makin's sure he ain't gonna be in the midst of thangs," said Adkins.

"Think he's a bit on the yeller side?" asked Haywood Tenkiller.

"Well, let's say he may not be a chicken, but he has his hen house ways."

"I'd say," agreed Tenkiller with a grin.

"Lane, if'n you'll build us a fire while you're restin', I'll brew up the coffee…What say?" asked Big Floyd.

"Dangnation. I take you to raise, Adkins?" asked Doyle, aka Jack McGann.

"Not yet, but somebody's got to do it…Reed, you want to give him a hand gatherin' some blow-down an' deadfall?…Don't git no green stuff. Smokes too much."

"'Peers that's the only way we're gonna git any coffee an' beans an' bacon," said Lane.

He turned to a skinny as a rail outlaw. "Let's go, Tall Jim, ain't gonna git done by itself."

Thirty minutes later, there was a good fire going inside a circle of rocks. Big Floyd had set the coffee pot on a flat rock next to the blaze.

Doyle was stirring a couple cans of beans with some bacon in a skillet on another rock.

"You decide if'n we're havin' beans an' bacon er bacon an' beans, Lane?" asked Ugly George.

"Well, since ya'll didn't seem to like the beans an' bacon last night, figured I'd switch it to bacon an' beans with some hot water cornbread," replied Doyle.

"Hell, gittin' adventuresome, ain'tcha?" commented Tenkiller.

"Yeah, I git tired of the same ol' thing, too…But, somebody else gits to clean up…Believe it's 'bout yer turn, ain't it, Marquis?" said Lane.

"Naw, done it last night…it's Ruiz' turn."

"Oh, gringo, but you do eet so well…But, for chu, I do eet this time."

Bass and Bone watched the men having their after dinner coffee sitting around the camp from a thick copse of cedars.

Lane threw a couple more large limbs on the fire causing a shower of sparks to swirl up into the moonless night.

Little Dime, aka Brushy Bill, made a point to keep his eyes away from the fire as did Big Floyd and Lane Doyle.

"Nice of them to build such a nice bright fire for us so we could find their camp," said Bone, sotto voce.

"Uh, huh." Bass grinned. "That's Jack's doin's. That wuz him throwin' those logs on the fire."

"Figured it was. The big guy and the small fellow and Jack are making it a point to not look at the fire."

"That's Selden and Brushy Bill...They know it ruins their night vision...Looks like they've got a place off downstream to get rid of their coffee an' erect monuments," whispered Bass.

"I think we can help with that by scarin' the pee out of them down there, don't you?"

Bass chuckled softly. "I'd say. This area is kindly knowd fer bein' a mite spooky...Many folks just plain disappear in this wilderness...not to say nothin' 'bout the bears, panthers an' the *Lofa*."

"What's a *Lofa*?" asked Bone.

"A legendary big hairy man-beast."

"Oh, we just call them Big Foot. The Indians in the northwest call them *Sasquach*...All means the same...You got them here, huh?"

Bass nodded.

"Ever seen one?"

Bass cut his eyes to Bone and nodded again.

§§§

CHAPTER EIGHTEEN

GATES CREEK

Flynn had built a hat-sized fire for their supper and coffee. He dug a ten inch hole and lined the top with rocks from the creek to bank the fire and cut down the glow. The dry wood he used almost eliminated any smoke. What little there was, dispersed in the canopied foliage overhead.

BONE

They had finished eating the rabbit stew with potatoes and wild onions Flynn had made. Loraine was in charge of the coffee and made a fresh pot of the stout trail brew. Newton lay near the fire pit, chewing on rabbit bones and left over hot water cornbread dodgers.

"Coffee's hot, who needs some?" Loraine asked.

Everyone, including Lucy, held up their cups.

"Thought you'd never ask," commented the Shaman, Doctor Ashalatubbi, as he held his out. "Getting a mite chilly."

Loraine filled everyone's cup and set the pot back on the flat rock next to the fire to keep it warm. She sat down, leaned back against a washtub-sized rock and lifted her cup to take a sip.

A piercing woman-like scream reverberated through the valley. Loraine also screamed and spilled some of her coffee.

"My God! What was that," she said as she dropped her cup, jumped to her feet, drew her .45. and looked out at the dark woods.

"That, my dear, was the ubiquitous large cat known as a cougar, puma, mountain lion or panther and sometimes catamount," commented *Anompoli Lawa*.

The echoes of the panther scream were followed by a deep throaty roar in the distance and two loud tree knocks.

Newton was on his feet, staring out into the dark woods, a deep growl rumbled in his throat. The hair along his back was standing up.

Loraine looked at the Shaman and then at Flynn. "Then what was that?"

Doctor Ashalatubbi arched his brows a little in surprise. "Well, that would undoubtedly be the *Lofa*...Wild man of the forest...A giant hairy ape-like creature that has roamed these woods since the Great Spirit, *Chí-hóo-wah,* fought with the fire-breathing horned devil and kicked him out of Heaven."

"They've been here since we started coming to your planet, Terra, many millennia ago," said Lucy. "They are a branch or subspecies of the hominoids that took a different direction in the evolutionary process...Well, actually, we just didn't pick their line when we stimulated your homo sapiens species with some of our genes starting about fifty thousand of your years ago."

"That would be about the time our cave dwelling ancestors started making tools and drawing pictures on the walls of their caves," said the doctor.

"The ability to create, especially in construction, tools, music and art is one of the first harbingers of civilization…Our genes planted the seed for that."

"You mean your DNA, Lucy?" said Loraine.

"Excuse me…the what?" asked Winchester.

"Oh, I'm sorry…DNA won't be discovered until, 1953…I forgot." Loraine turned to the doctor. "Deoxyribonucleic acid…It determines what makes us a person…our eye color, sex, hair, physical characteristics…Everything except our soul or spirit…Everyone's a little different."

"Indeed," said Doctor Ashalatubbi. "An outgrowth of Darwin's theory of evolution, I would surmise…What Mendel described as *genetics* in 1866 and Miescher identified with *nuclein* in 1869."

"That's very good *Anompoli Lawa*," said Lucy.

"Actually, Lucy, we studied their findings in medical school," he said, almost embarrassed. "Although no one really knew what the two men were talking about." He chuckled.

"We use it in police work in our time to identify criminals in crime scene investigations...Blood, hair, tissue, saliva, semen, and so on," added Loraine.

"Not to change the subject, but, do you think those creatures will try to come into our camp?" asked Flynn.

Doctor Ashalatubbi shook his head. "Oh, not really. Not withstanding the legends, the *Lofa* are normally quite shy...They just give out warnings and knock on trees with big sticks to inform humans and other predators to stay away...They bluff, in other words."

"I hope they know that," muttered Loraine as she glanced into the stygian darkness again as two more tree knocks sounded.

"That sounded close," commented Flynn.

A waning gibbous moon had just cleared the tree tops when Pedro Ruiz got to his feet, pitched the dregs left in his coffee cup in the fire and headed downstream. The only sounds in the dark woods were the normal cacophony of night music supplied by crickets, cicadas, frogs and night owls.

"Looks like the Mexican needs to drain his lizard," commented Bone as they watched from a place of concealment in persimmon thicket near the outlaw's camp. "Let's follow him."

"Lead on, o big white warrior," whispered Bass with a grin.

They followed Ruiz downstream along a game trail that ran alongside the rock-bottomed, clear water creek. The three inch rowel jingle-bob spurs on his black knee-high boots jangled as he walked.

Pedro was the most ostentatious of the gang. A real gunhawk in the traditional Mexican style. His outfit consisted of black, tight-fitting pants with silver conchos down the outside of each leg and a matching waist-length, fitted jacket with silver embroidery, known as a Bolero jacket, or sometimes a Roundabout. His black silver-stitched sombrero hung down his back by a braided *barbiquejo*.

A black silver concho and stud decorated gunbelt was strapped low around his hips with a mother-of-pearl handled Colt Peacemaker in cross-draw on his left side and a wicked looking stag-handled ten inch Bowie on the right—both of which he knew how to use.

When he reached his destination, he unbuckled his gunbelt to get to the buttons down the front of his trousers. He hung the belt and holster on a limb to his right.

He was watering a bush with a long drawn out sigh at the relief of draining his full bladder when his chrome-plated .45 lifted from the holster beside his head almost as if by magic.

"*Madre de Dios!*" He whirled about as the hammer moved back to full cock with two ominous clicks in the still night and the barrel leveled at his face. His member lost some of its turgidity, shriveled up and drew back into his leather trousers where it continued to drain his bladder.

"*Fantasma...espíritu!*" he whispered.

His eyes were big as saucers as they searched the dim moonlit darkness in the heavy surrounding woods for some sign of a person.

"What do you do in my country?" asked a disembodied voice.

"*¿Quién...quién eres?*...Who...who are you?" Ruiz stammered.

"I am the spirit of the Seven Devils and you violate my sanctity," said the voice. "You will die…You all will die." A malevolent laugh rumbled from the darkness.

"*No! No! Por favor…Lo siento. No te quise lastimar.*" Pedro dropped to his knees.

"You lie! You have come to harm."

"No! *En la tumba de mi madre santa.*"

"You not only disrespect the spirits of the Seven Devils, but your mother, also."

"*Por favor…me iré ahora.*"

"You will leave my land or die where you stand…Go back to your country and never come here again."

"*Sí, me iré ahora…¿Puedo tener mi arma…mi pistola.*"

The voice laughed again. "Just go…Now! Or you will not live to see the morrow," the spirit hissed.

The muzzle pressed against his forehead hard enough to leave a deep circular impression in the skin.

"*Sí, sí, Pedro va.*"

He turned and ran back up the trail to the camp and started gathering his silver decorated saddle, saddlebags and soogan.

"What are you doin', Ruiz?" asked Snake Smith.

"Pedro leaves this cursed country," he said as he turned to go to get his horse.

"What in hell for?" asked Evil Carl. "You ain't been paid yet."

He looked over his shoulder. "Dead men need no money...*No se puede luchar contra fantasmas.*"

"What do you mean, ghosts?...And where's your iron?" asked Bull.

All the others were on their feet.

He stopped, turned, faced the gang and spoke rapidly. "*Espíritu se lo llevó. Dijo que dejar su país o morir. Todo morirá.*"

"Dammit, Pedro, speak English," said Snake as he spat into the fire.

Ruiz paused and took a breath. "The spirit of the Seven Devils took it...Said to leave hees country...All will die! We will all surely die!" Pedro disappeared down the trail to where the horses were picketed.

The rest of the outlaws looked fearfully and with no small degree of trepidation out into the blackness surrounding their camp.

The woods went completely silent, and then a loud roar sounded from upstream followed by three loud tree knocks.

Bone touched two turquoise stones on his bracelet. The air shimmered slightly and he became visible to Bass again.

The two men looked at each other as the echoes of the primal scream died away.

"*Lofa?*" said Bone.

"*Lofa*," concurred Bass.

"Well, didn't plan that, but it damn sure is helping. Those hoodlums will be looking over their shoulders and jumping at every unusual sound each step they take," said Bone with his patented grin.

They watched as the outlaws, except for Jack, Selden and Brushy Bill, looked around and nervously moved closer to the fire. The three undercover law officers surreptitiously exchanged glances and wry grins before heading to their bedrolls.

Bill leaned close to Jack as they walked and whispered, "Bass?"

Jack looked at him and raised one eyebrow. "Damn, I hope so."

"Great balls of fire," exclaimed Roosevelt as he got to his feet from his place next to the campfire. "I know the first scream was a mountain lion...but, what in the Sam Hill was the other?"

"I'm sure I don't know, sir," said Marvin Wilhite, the gun bearer, as he stared out into the gloomy forest. There was a late evening ground fog rolling in through the woods from the nearby creek.

"Bring me Betsy."

"Yes, sir."

Wilhite went to the area where he had unrolled his bedroll and opened the guncase containing Roosevelt's favorite hunting rifle. It was an engraved Winchester Model 1886, chambered in .45-90, suitable for big-game—custom made for him by Winchester Arms. It had an oval gold nameplate engraved with his name and the Roosevelt crest embedded in the stock.

The young man carried it back over to Roosevelt and handed it to him along with the oil impregnated cleaning cloth he always required.

Teddy looked at him over the top of the pince-nez glasses perched on his nose. "Cartridges,

Marvin, I need cartridges," Teddy said as he took the rifle.

"Oh, yes, sir. Of course."

He trotted back over to the hunting gear, grabbed a box of the long .45-90 rounds, headed back and handed them to Roosevelt.

"Thank you, son...Don't ever bring me a weapon without ammunition...Understand?"

Teddy began inserting the brass cartridges into the side port of the iconic weapon.

"You're loading it, sir?" asked Marvin.

Roosevelt looked up again with a steely glare. "Gun's not much good empty, is it, Mister Wilhite?"

"Yes, sir...Uh, no, sir," he answered, properly chastised, as the panther screamed again.

§§§

CHAPTER NINETEEN

GATES CREEK, WEST SIDE

"Got'ny coffee left," asked Bass as he and Bone entered the camp from a thick copse of fog enshrouded cedars on the back side.

"Dangnation, Bass, ya'll are like ghosts," said Bodie as he spun around.

"Can't believe Spot didn't smell you coming," commented Fiona, looking up from where she was squatting down by the fire.

"Come from downwind, Marshal. Knowed he'd catch our scent if we didn't," said Bass.

"We were practicing," added Bone.

"Don't know if you need any practice," said Fiona with a smile as she added a couple of pieces of deadfall to the blaze.

Bass glanced at Bone. "Big feller here is purty dang good at movin' through the woods on the quiet."

"I'm better in rough mountain country like it was over in Afghanistan…And love these buckskins and moccasins."

"Where's Af-ghan-is-tan?" asked Bass.

"It's the middle east…north of India and east of Egypt and Israel…you know, the area where Isaac, Moses and Jesus were," said Fiona.

"Oh, like in the Bible?"

"Thought you couldn't read, Bass," said Bone.

"Cain't…But, used to listen to Jack read from it an' other books like Shakespeare, Keats, Browning, an' them wrote…I 'member most ever thing I hear er see."

"Ah, you have a photographic memory," commented Bone.

"Don't know what that is, but, I sees everthang as picturs, like tracks an' that's what I 'member…An' what I hears, I makes a pictur in my head an' 'member stories an' such thataway."

"Good a way as any," said Bone.

"I assume ya'll found the ambushers?" asked Fiona as she grabbed two cups and filled them from the pot next to the fire.

"We did," replied Bass as he took one of the cups and laughed. "Bone pertended he was a spirit, usin' that magic bracelet Lucy give 'im, an' skeered one 'em half to death…He lit a shuck back fer Mexico…That cuts 'em down to fourteen an' three of them is marshals."

"Well, that's eleven…Getting down to a manageable level," commented Bone, and then he grinned. "Science at a different time is often called…magic, Bass."

"That be true enough, I mind."

Fiona handed Bone the other filled cup.

"The strawboss an' one other is trailin' along behind. Overheered Selden an' some of them rannies sayin' that they thought he was a tad yeller...'Spect we be a findin' out," said Bass as he blew across the top of his coffee and took a sip.

"Where's Flynn an' them?" asked Bodie.

Bass pointed with his free hand. "Yonderway, 'bout quarter mile east of the huntin' party."

"Let's see if we can capture that strawboss. Should be fairly easy since he'll be avoiding the main ambush..."

"Good idee, Bone. He could lead us an' the Secret Service to whoever's callin' the dance...Right now, we gots no clue other than that feller he met with in Paris what's one of the Congress Representatives fer north Texas."

"So you think the Congressman's working for someone, Bass?" asked Fiona.

"Ain't no question in my mind. Like most all them politicians...they's somebody with lots of money that's a trollin' 'em around."

Bone chuckled. "It's no different in our time, either...We have an expression we use. 'Follow the money trail'," he added. "Money equals power...Power equals control...Control equals money."

"Sounds like a big circle," said Bodie.

Bone looked at the ranger and grinned. "Now you have it."

"'He that wants money, means, and content is without three good friends', said Shakespeare in *As You Like It*," quoted Fiona.

"Tell ya'll what do, I'll go back an' work with Flynn on they side...Bone, you an' Fiona take them nabobs on this side...I mind they'll be six to the side...Jack an' Selden be in the west group, Brushy Bill in the east."

"What about the two behind, Bass?" asked Fiona.

"Bodie, you drop back an' take care of them two. Jest don't kill the strawboss...We be a needin' him, I 'spect," said Bass.

"Sounds easy enough," commented Bodie.

GATES CREEK, EAST SIDE

"Good evening, Bass," said Lucy without looking up from the skillet filled with thick slices of sizzling bacon sitting on a flat rock next to the fire.

"Ain't no slippin' up on you, is they, little missy?"

She smiled. "Not likely. You're like a beacon in the night, Bass." Lucy got to her feet and moved the cooked bacon away from the fire and glanced over at the dog laying nearby. "Even Newton didn't sound an alarm."

Bass chuckled. "He knowed it was me."

"Dogs sense the presence of a person in addition to catching the scent," said Lucy.

"This little lady continues to amaze me," said Doctor Ashalatubbi as he sipped on his coffee.

"So what's your plan, Bass?" asked Flynn.

"Well, Sheriff, you an' me er gonna take the ridge on the southeast side of the pass an' try to git above where them outlaws is gonna be…"

"Bass, we're being watched," commented Lucy.

Newton was on his feet, peering out into the fog cloaked darkness, and growling, his hair rose up along his back.

Without looking up, Bass commented, "Man?"

Lucy glanced at the big marshal as he squatted down beside the fire to fill his cup. "No."

Doctor Ashalatubbi set his cup down, picked up his rifle and levered a round in the chamber.

"I don't sense any aggression, right now, *Anompoli Lawa*, said Lucy.

The morning fog slowly lifted as the sun broke above the horizon on the other side of the Seven Devil Hills. A red sky with golden arrows streaking from the east heralded the possibility of a storm later in the day.

Tarlton Brewster stood in the center of the camp next to the fire as the early morning temperature in the hills was a little cool. He took a sip of his coffee and looked around at the men under his charge.

"Awright boys, you all have your assignments. Start pickin' Roosevelt's entourage off as they come into view."

"You still goin' to be back behind in case they make a break back to the river?" asked Tenkiller.

"Shore, no need in lettin' 'em out of the trap, now is there?…'Sides they shouldn't panic if ya'll do what yer tol' an' pop them city boys one at the time as they move up Gates Creek into the heart of the Seven Devils."

"What about that spirit Ruiz wus babblin' 'bout 'fore he pulled out last night?" asked Snake Smith.

"Haw! That greaser jest got cold feet was all," Brewster answered as he glanced over at Tobacca Bob for support.

The small, wormy looking, outlaw spat an amber stream into the fire where it popped and sizzled on a burning cedar limb and nodded.

"Well, you weren't here, Brewster. That Mex was skeered out of his wits…Ain't never seen him skeered of 'nything 'fore an' I've rid with him a long time," said Marquis Rudabaugh.

"So you say…Enough of this whinin', ya'll split up an' take yer positions. Don't want to see 'nybody else git chicken livered…Now git gone." Brewster pitched what was left of his coffee to the ground and he and Tobacca Bob headed for their horses.

"Chicken livered, my ass," mumbled Tenkiller as Brewster and Bob rode out of sight through the trees. "Sumbitch oughta look in a mirror…ask me."

Tall Jim nodded at Big Floyd, aka Marshal Selden Lindsey, and his men and they also headed to their mounts.

It was past midmorning as Tall Jim positioned his men in the trees northwest of the trail along Gates Creek.

"Know this country, had a place near here used to use fer a hideout. Snake there's a barrel sized boulder down by the creek. Good place to see 'em comin'...You git first shot

"Need one of us to go along?" asked Little Dime Williams.

"Naw, be fine," said Snake.

Little Dime pursed his lips and frowned as he watched Smith ride off down the narrow game trail.

Tall Jim scattered his men on the northeast side, placing them where they didn't have the best angles on the trail below.

"Dang, Jim, ain't got a very good openin' to shoot through," complained Bull.

"Also means they cain't see to shoot back at you, numnuts."

"Oh, right," Bull said as he snuggled up behind a foot thick sycamore.

BONE

Possum Middens led Roosevelt's party up the southeast side of Gates Creek toward its headwaters in the Kiamichi Mountains. Reginald Baker was behind him some ten yards leading one of the pack mules.

Roosevelt assistant, Frank Warren was tracking behind Baker with another of the pack mules when a shot rang out from the opposite side of the creek.

Warren yelled out, threw his hands up in the air and pitched sideways to the ground beside his horse. The startled mule brayed, kicked his back feet up in the air and bolted up the trail past Middens.

"Everybody down," yelled Roosevelt from back down the trail as he bailed from his horse with his Winchester.

The rest of his assistants including his gun bearer, Marvin Wilhite, immediately dismounted and sought protection. He took cover behind a cottonwood tree next to the creek.

"Where'd that shot come from, Middens?" shouted Teddy at the guide hiding behind a boulder along the side of the trail.

"Think it come from cross the creek," he answered.

"Don't see no smoke," added Baker. "Maybe it was a stray shot through the woods from a hunter."

Another shot rang out and the sickening *twack* of a bullet striking flesh followed immediately. Wilhite pitched forward on his face from behind the tree.

"That shot came from the opposite direction," yelled Secret Service agent Thomas, crouching down behind a pecan tree and looking behind him, and then across the creek.

"I think that eliminates the possibility of an errant shot by a hunter," said Roosevelt as he levered a round into the chamber of his Winchester and tried to spot a telltale cloud of white smoke...

§§§

CHAPTER TWENTY

SEVEN DEVIL HILLS

A long, rolling peal of thunder echoed across the Kiamichi Mountains from the west. The thickening, boiling, dark clouds overhead began to take on an ominous green tinged look. A flash of cloud to cloud lightning created another extended rumble of thunder like a distant artillery battle.

Bass and Bone moved silently through the woods on their respective sides of the creek looking for the two hidden shooters.

Bone caught a glimpse of Boone Prescott, behind a large boulder with his Winchester. He quietly slipped up behind him with his Bowie in his right hand, drove his knee into the middle of the killer's back and grabbed the front of his hair. Pulling his head back, Bone made a quick slash across the assassin's neck, severing his carotid artery and the windpipe. Air hissed from Prescott's open throat as the blood spurted, covering the side of the tree.

Bone released his hair, let him slump to the leaf-covered ground like a pile of dirty laundry and watched as his left foot drummed briefly against the leaf strewn forest floor in his death throes. "You won't murder anyone else."

He looked up through the foliage over his head at the churning clouds and smelled the coming rain in the air.

"Damn."

Bass moved like a ghost through the trees and squatted down behind the outlaw that had just shot Wilhite from behind the sycamore tree on the east side of Gates Creek near the trail.

"You be Snake Smith I takes it," said Reeves softly.

"Jesus!" exclaimed the gunhawk as he rolled over and pointed his cocked Winchester directly at Bass. "Damn, nigger…Who the hell are you?"

Reeves grinned. "Well, some folks calls me one thing, some call me 'nother…But, most calls me Bass Reeves…Deputy United States Marshal, Bass Reeves."

"Reeves?…Oh, God."

"…an' I gots paper on you Harry *Snake* Smith, fer murder, larceny of horses, armed robbery, an' rape…'Peers as though you jest added to yer list." He chuckled. "'Course they cain't hangs you but onct…Pity."

"The hell you say…I got my rifle pointed at yer gut, darkie, an' all I gotta do is pull the trigger," said Snake as he got up. "You can kiss yer black ass good bye." The fear of facing the legendary Bass Reeves was obvious in his eyes.

Bass also rose to his feet and chuckled again. "Uh, huh...But I mind this jest ain't gonna be yer day, rannie...Now, as I sees it, you gots two choices...Put down that shooter an' I'll take you in fer trial...er die where you stand." Bass shrugged his shoulders. "Yer choice."

"Haw...You stupid damned..."

Smith never finished what he was going to say as one of Bass' crossdraw .38-40 Colts appeared almost as if by magic in his right hand and roared in the quietness of the deep woods of the Seven Devil Hills. A rumble of thunder overhead sounded almost like an echo of the shot.

A cloud of white smoke billowed in front of Bass as a pencil-sized hole appeared just below the brim of Snake's hat, snapping his head back.

A surprised look came over the outlaw's face as a small rivulet of blood trickled down the side of his nose. Smith's eyes clicked back in his head as he collapsed to the ground like so much wet newspaper.

Bone grinned and nodded as the single pistol shot sounded from across the creek. ".38-40...Bass."

"They're shooting again…Stay down," yelled Thomas as he looked up the hill behind them.

"That was a handgun, Wesley, and it wasn't in this direction…Middens, is there anyplace we can take cover?" yelled Roosevelt from his hide. "Looks like this is going to be what we call back in New England a 'nor'easter', but in this case a 'nor'wester'."

"We jest call it a frog strangler, Mister Roosevelt, and yep there's a small cave just up yonder couple hundert yards."

"What about Warren and Wilhite's bodies?" Teddy asked.

"Have to leave 'em fer now…no time. Storm's comin' too fast…both have bought the farm, anyhoo," said Middens.

Fiona glanced up as the big man slipped back to the group.

"Bone let's get everybody over underneath that overhang on that outcrop. I think it's the best we're going to be able to do," she said as the first downdraft of cool air whipped through the trees.

"Sounds good to me," he replied. "Let's go."

Bone followed Fiona and Bodie, leading their horses, over to the overhang on the granite outcrop to their west.

"Everybody git out yer slickers er ground tarps. Gonna have to rig us up a shelter," shouted Bass over the sound of the rising wind already bending the tree tops overhead as he rushed back through the woods to the others.

Flynn and Bass quickly tied the tarps together with rawhide pigging strings, and then stretched them between two eight inch black gum trees—their leaves were just beginning to turn bright red for the fall. They pulled the back edge down to the ground and tacked it with picket pins and rocks and created a makeshift lean-to against the direction of the storm.

Bass and Flynn hobbled the horses with Doctor Ashalatubbi's help as Loraine gathered some deadfall to put under the tarps to keep it dry.

"They'll turn they butts to the wind an' git up under some of them big trees...Be awright."

"Everyone get tight around me under the tarps and I'll activate a field around us which will protect us from the hail and blowing rain," instructed Lucy as they stuffed their saddles and food packs at the back of the lean-to.

Flynn, Bass, Doctor Ashalatubbi, Loraine and Newton crawled underneath and surrounded Lucy as big drops of rain began to fall through the trees. She touched a couple of the turquoise stones inset in the solid gold links in her bracelet. The air around them shimmered and the water started rolling off the force field to the ground.

"Well if this ain't the dangdest thang," said Bass.

"Amazing, absolutely amazing," added *Anompoli Lawa.*

"Son of a gun," said Flynn as he watched the rain run off her field like it was a window pane.

"I've seen Bone use his several times and it still freaks me out," commented Loraine.

Lightning crashed overhead and marble-sized hail began to pepper down, knocking leaves and small limbs to the ground. The ice stones bounced from the lean-to and the part of Lucy's field that extended out from under the tarps.

After fifteen minutes, the hail stopped, leaving the ground with a thin coat of white—but the rain continued in a pounding deluge, rapidly melting the small round chunks of ice.

"Can't see three feet through that," said Loraine over the roar of the downpour.

"Good thing we be a right smart piece above the creek. It's liable to git purty high. The whole valley gonna be under water...Seen it afore in this wilderness," commented Bass. "Good thing is, she'll go down 'bout as fast as she went up."

"Long as it doesn't get up to the camp first," said Loraine.

After thirty minutes, the heavy downpour slacked off down to a steady rain of about another fifteen minutes, and then to a heavy drizzle. Gates Creek below was already out of its banks and rising.

"Good thing it's still daylight...Water did like to have reached our camp when Jack an' I wuz bringin' the Trotter gang out over twelve year ago...It wuz night time an' the water wuz lappin' at the edge of our camp when the sun come up." Bass chuckled. "We wuz over a hundert feet from the creek bank when we got under our tarps."

"Looks like it's slackin' off some. Glad Loraine put some kindlin' under the tarp before it started…Might need a fire tonight after the storm," said Flynn.

"When she slacks off a little more, could be a fair time to slip upon them ambusher's camp on this side…Mind they'll be huddled up outta the rain like us," said Bass.

"Could be you're right, Marshal…How many you reckon is left on this side?" asked Flynn.

Bass scratched the stubble on his chin. "Well, Snake Smith wadn't inclined to give his self up, an' Jack and Marshal Lindsey is part of that group…So I makes it they's two of the miscreants left…God help 'em."

"Think Selden an' Jack can take care of 'em?" asked Flynn.

Bass nodded. "Reckon so…an' that's a good point, Sheriff…Mind they'll give 'em the same choices I give Snake Smith…an' probably with the same results."

"Yep, neither of them is inclined to cut killers much slack…what I understand," said Flynn.

"I can vouch for that," commented Doctor Ashalatubbi. "Good a lawmen as there are in the Nations...even if one of them is my nephew...well, acquired nephew through his wife, Angie."

"How high's that water, Middens?" asked Teddy.

"'Bout twenty feet below the cave, Mister Roosevelt."

"Horses all right?"

"Might send someone to check 'em 'fore dark," Possum replied. "Now that the rain has slowed down some."

"Harvey, why don't you slip down the way and see to our animals. You have your slicker on."

"Yessir, Mister Roosevelt," the assistant responded.

"I'll go with him," said the guide. "Case 'ny of the hobbles need adjustin'."

As Bass and Flynn discussed, Marshals McGann and Lindsey decided to make their move on the remaining two outlaws on their own.

The four men were huddled against a vertical thrust fault of gray granite sticking up about thirty feet from the side of the ridge.

Jack and Selden had positioned themselves on each side of the outlaws—they exchanged knowing glances. McGann eased his S & W Russian revolver from his holster and looked over at Tall Jim, his long frame was scrunched up against the rock.

"You know, Jim, just to let you an' Evil Carl there know, Big Floyd an' me 're actually Deputy US Marshals Selden Lindsey an' Jack McGann…an' you fellers 're under arrest." Jack grinned. "Don't that make yer day?"

"What?" said Tall Jim, jerking up and looking over at Big Floyd, aka, Marshal Lindsey, also holding his handgun on the pair.

"Huh?" added Evil Carl glancing first at Selden, and then at Jack. "Ya'll 're funnin' us."

"Not hardly, nabob, you heered right. You boys have crapped an' fell back in it," said Selden as he thumbed the hammer on his Colt.

"What 're we gonna do with these halfwits, Selden? Gonna put a fly in the buttermilk when we go to join Bass an' them gittin' the other bunch…Reckon we oughta jest shoot 'em?" asked Jack.

"Now wait a minute, wait a minute…We ain't done nothin', yet," complained Tall Jim.

"Naw, naw…we wuz jest 'long fer the paycheck. We wadn't gonna shoot nobody," added Carl.

"So you say…But, we already know what evil lurks in yer minds an' hearts…I think you play false with us." Selden looked over at McGann. "Say, Jack, do we or Bass got 'ny paper on these two miscreants?"

"Not that I know 'bout…But, we know what they was fixin' to do…an' 'sides we done got 'em on accessory to murder, though," said Jack

"Fact." Lindsey paused for a moment, thinking. "Tell you what do."

"What?" asked Jim.

"You fellers shuck them irons an' any knives er hideouts you got…"

Jack interrupted Selden. "An' take off'n yer boots."

"Huh?" asked Evil Carl. "What fer?"

"Fer the reason we're gonna let you jackanapes go…if'n you git the hell out of the Nations…an' don't go to Texas neither," replied Jack.

"An' if we ever see you again…well, we'll jest shoot you on sight…Got that?" added Lindsey.

"You bet…We'll jest git our horses an' you badge toters'll never see hide, hair, ner tallow of us again…Ain't that right, Jim?"

"Damn straight."

"Nope, sorry boys, that ain't the way she's a gonna work," said Jack. "Now, git them boots off…like I said."

"Uh…How's it gonna work, then?" asked Carl as he and Jim pulled their boots off.

"Yer gonna scat outta here unarmed, shanks mare an' barefoot with jest what yer a wearin' on yer backs," added Selden. "Meby it'll convince you to change yer line of work."

"But, what about the bears, wolves an' panthers?" whined Tall Jim.

"Ain't our problem, slick." Jack got a wry grin on his mustachioed face, spat a stream of amber tobacco juice off to the side and chuckled. "How fast kin ya'll run?"

§§§

CHAPTER TWENTY-ONE

SEVEN DEVIL HILLS

Harvey and Possum Middens worked their way through the dripping trees and brush along a narrow game trail that bordered the raging Gates Creek. They reached the small glade on a flat area, that was now just above the water line, where the horses were hobbled on some late summer grass, grazing.

BONE

Harvey bent over and was checking the hobbles on the pack horse when Middens slipped up behind him, drew his Remington hit the young man on the side of his head.

The assistant collapsed to the ground with a grunt, unconscious.

The guide picked up Harvey by his heels and dragged him to the edge of the churning, flooded creek. He dropped him, and then rolled the inert form of the young man off the bank and into the churning, muddy water. IIis body rapidly disappeared into the fast moving creek.

Middens watched the water for a few moments until he was sure the body wasn't hung up on some underwater brush, and then he turned around, leaned against a pecan tree, rolled a quirley and had a smoke before he walked back to the cave.

Possum rushed back into the cave, bent over and put his hands on his knees, feigning being out of breath. "Mister Roosevelt! Mister Roosevelt! Harvey…He's gone…he's gone!"

Teddy shot to his feet. "What do you mean, man? He's gone where?"

"The creek, sir. He slipped an' fell into the water...It swallered him right up. I tried to reach him, but, weren't no use. The current was too strong...His body'll be down to the Red 'fore sundown...I'm shore sorry, sir, I liked the lad."

"Great Zeus! What next?" said Roosevelt as he stomped in a tight circle. "By the Lord Jim, there's no call for this."

"I'm powerful sorry, sir. I truly am," the guide said contritely.

He turned and stepped over to the fire at the mouth of the cave. A slight smile briefly crossed his face as he squatted down, wrapped one of his gloves around the handle of the hot coffee pot next to the fire and poured a cup of the hot trail brew.

The Secret Service agent, Wesley Thomas, glared at Middens as he blew across the surface of the coffee and took a sip.

The dusk of the gloaming had settled in to the Gates Creek valley as the light faded to red and purple arrows streaking across the darkening sky from the invisible sun just below the horizon. The cloud cover moved off to the east.

"Halloo, the camp," shouted Jack through the trees.

"That you, Jack?" answered Bass.

"Damn, I hope so, Bass. Either that er I stole his stuff."

"Selden with you?" he asked.

"Yep...Comin' in," Jack replied.

He and Marshal Lindsey led their horses into the small clearing.

"About time, nephew," said *Anompoli Lawa*.

"Sorry, Uncle, we had a little bidness to take care of."

"The fact that ya'll 're here tells me this side is clear," said Flynn.

"Close enough," replied Selden.

"Ya'll take yer horses yonderway through the trees. They's a clearin' with some good late summer grass you kin picket 'em on...'long with our'n," said Bass. "We'll make a fresh pot...If'n ya'll want some?"

"Thought you'd never ask," answered Jack.

They led their mounts on down the narrow game trail just above the turbid creek to the glade Bass mentioned, stripped their tack, and rubbed the horses down with a piece of burlap. After letting them drink from the swollen creek, they fed them a couple of handfuls of grain and headed back to the camp with their soogans, rifles and saddlebags.

"Just barely run mine over, Bass," said Jack as he and Selden walked up to the fire in front of the lean-to the group had built before the storm after setting down their traps.

"You kin git yer own dang coffee, Jack, didn't take ya'll to raise," quipped Bass.

"That's gratitude for ya," said Selden as he grabbed the pot with his folded over bandana and poured a cup for himself and Jack.

"Don't see no prisoners…Ya'll have to kill them other two?" asked Bass.

"Nope, didn't have no paper on 'em so we let 'em go."

"Let them go?" exclaimed Doctor Ashalatubbi.

Selden and Jack exchanged glances and grins.

"Without their guns, horses or boots," replied Jack.

"Ooh, that's mean…but humane." Lucy laughed.

"Quickest way I know of to get miscreants to change their attitudes…Can humble the meanest of 'em," commented Selden after he licked the edge of his cup and took a sip of the hot stout liquid.

"That's something Bone would do," said Loraine with a grin from her seat on a rock. "He might have made them lose their pants, too.

"Dang, wish we'd of thought 'bout that…Told 'em to get out of the Nations an' not go to Texas neither…or they'd suffer their death next time we seen 'em," added Jack. "They whined a mite 'bout bein' unarmed and barefoot…but saw that it was better than the alternative purty quick like."

"Snake Smith wadn't inclined to discuss the matter…God rest his soul," said Bass as he refreshed his cup.

"Committed suicide by lawman, did he?" commented Jack.

"Could say," replied Bass.

"Don't believe I know this little lady an' who's Bone?" asked Selden.

"Tell you when he gits in…They're together. Same story," said Bass.

"Ya'll may find it hard to believe," added Winchester with a smile.

"You say so," replied Jack.

"What are we havin' for supper, Jack?…Believe it's your turn to fix," asked Flynn.

"Well, how's 'bout cat's ass an' cabbage?…That suit you?" replied Jack with a wry grin.

"With or without cornbread?" inquired Flynn.

Loraine got to her feet. "Never mind…I'll fix supper. None of ya'll can cook worth a wooden nickel, anyway."

"Uh, huh," Jack said with a smile as he picked up the pot and filled his cup. "Figured that'd work.

"Believe it's pretty well over, don't ya'll?" commented Bone as he looked up through the still dripping foliage overhead as traces of blue streaked with red from the setting sun started to show on the back side of the front.

"Looks like," said Bodie.

"Think Bass and them got their side cleaned up?"

"Considering it was Bass Reeves, Selden Lindsey and Jack McGann against only five of the malefactors…I feel confident they have, Bone," said Fiona.

"Then we got work to do. Don't think either us or our group are crossin' the creek for the next day or so," commented Bodie.

"But, on the other hand, they can't get to Mister Roosevelt's party either," added Fiona.

"Which side do you think the straw boss an' the other feller are?" asked Bodie.

"No telling. I suspect you'll have to go scouting in the morning," said Fiona.

"I'll go find them tonight, Bodie...It's my thing," added Bone. "Now, I'm hungry, how about ya'll?"

"If ya'll can find some dry kindling and semidry deadfall, I'll start supper," offered Fiona.

Bone walked to the edge of the small clearing to a standing dead cottonwood, stuck his knife under the bark on the east side and pried a large slab off. He turned it over and scraped most of the dry fibrous cambium from the inside with his fingernails and rolled it between his massive hands. In a moment, the fibers were almost a powder.

He went to an open spot, dug a quick hole in the damp forest floor with his knife, laid a large piece of the bark on the bottom outside down and placed the powdered punk on top.

"Ranger, are you going to just stand there or you going to go out and find some deadfall?" asked Bone.

"Oh, right…That's a good trick there."

"No trick…Just part of the survival training I went through in the Marine Corps." He began to strip some more of the bark off the tree, break it up into kindling and built a small teepee over the pile of punk. "Sometime today, slick," he said.

Bodie reached up and grabbed some of the branches left on the same tree, broke them off, and then snapped them into shorter pieces over his knee and handed them to Bone. "This'll do for starters while I go get some larger blowdown."

"Works for me," said Bone as he pulled the Bic lighter he always carried and held it close to the punk.

In a couple of seconds, the light brown powder began to smoke and then burst into a yellow flame. It quickly started the chunks of bark, and then the branches Bodie had brought.

"Have a cookin' fire shortly, Fiona," said Bone.

"Wonderful," she handed him the blue enameled graniteware coffee pot. "If you'll get some water, I'll start with some hot nectar of the gods for this cool, damp evening." She grinned showing her even white teeth.

BONE

"Don't think I can stand it," Bone quipped as he headed for the creek.

The morning broke clear and crisp over the Kiamichi Mountains along with the sweet smell of recently rain-washed air.

Teddy Roosevelt was first up in the camp, had built a fire, brewed a pot of coffee and was having a cup while standing on the bank, staring at the dropping water level in the creek.

Secret Service agent, Wesley Thomas walked up and stood beside him with his own coffee, interrupting his reverie.

"Oh, good morning, Thomas. How did you sleep?" Roosevelt asked, turning slightly.

"Not well, sir."

"Nor did I...Wrestled most of the night with trying to get a grasp on this situation...Three of my people dead...Makes no sense." He shook his head and took a sip from his cup.

"Maybe it does, sir."

Teddy turned to Wesley, looking at him over the top of his pince-nez glasses. "How so?"

"What if a group of people wanted to see that you didn't come back from this hunting trip?"

"What on earth for?"

Thomas paused for a long minute, glanced back at Middens, still in his bedroll, and then turned back to Roosevelt. "We, meaning the Secret Service, have reason to believe that you are the focus of a kidnapping plot."

"Oh, you jest, sir."

"I wish I were. We've got three Deputy US Marshals undercover with a gang of outlaws we think are in the Kiamichi Mountains here for that very purpose...I think the death of two of your assistants is a good indication that we're right...not to mention Harvey...uh, *accidentally* falling in the creek." He raised his eyebrows and cocked his head.

"My God in Heaven." Roosevelt turned his attention back to the flooded creek. "Why?...For money?"

"Not directly, sir."

"Then what?"

"We think it's political...Just not to what end," said Thomas.

"I'm just the Assistant Secretary of the Navy."

"Yes, sir, I know. That's why we joined forces with the office of the United States Marshal. They put five of their best on the case."

"Who?"

"Deputy Marshals Jack McGann, Fiona Mae Flynn, Bill Roberts, Selden Lindsey, Sheriff Mason Flynn from Jack County, Texas…and Bass Reeves."

Roosevelt nodded and pitched the remains of his coffee in the creek with a slight smile. "Bully…With Reeves involved, God help those high binders…because he won't. I've heard the US Marshal's office think he's their best Deputy."

"Yes, sir, that's why he's heading up the task force…He'll get to the bottom of this, rest assured of that…Additionally, there's one other law officer participating, from Texas, who is probably going to be of a great help…Name's Bone."

"Bone? Interesting name."

"You don't know the half of it, sir," replied the agent with a smile

"Oh?"

"I prefer he and his partner, Loraine Rodriguez to explain their presence."

"Another woman in addition to Deputy Marshal Fiona Flynn?"

Thomas grinned and nodded…

§§§

CHAPTER TWENTY-TWO

SEVEN DEVIL HILLS

Bodie rolled out of his bedroll, stretched, pulled on his cavalry style boots, stomped his feet to the bottom and stood up. "Any coffee?" he asked Fiona who had gotten up earlier and rebuilt the fire.

He looked over at Bone, also just getting out of his blankets. "Thought you were going to scout out the two bad guys back down the trail?"

The big man glanced at him and grinned. "Did." Bone finished lacing his tall Apache style moccasins up the side and got to his feet.

"Didn't know you left or when you came back," commented Fiona as she poured two cups of the stout trail brew and held them out to the men.

Bone smiled as he walked over and took his cup. "I know." He took a sip. "Mmm…Thank you, Fiona, you make great coffee."

She smiled back and tilted her head. "I know."

"Touché." Bone nodded at her and grinned again.

"So, what's the deal? They on this side or the other?" asked Bodie.

"Other…When do you think that water will be down low enough for us to cross?" Bone inquired.

Bodie glanced at the creek. "Already dropped near ten feet. 'Magine by this afternoon or evenin'should be down to belly deep on a horse…if it don't rain again.

Fiona looked at both horizons. "Well, I don't think we're going to get anymore rain anytime soon."

BONE

Reginald Baker walked back into camp buttoning up his canvas trousers after taking his morning constitutional. He abruptly stopped less than five feet into the clearing and knelt down to study the ground. "Mister Roosevelt, I think you should come take a look at this."

Teddy turned from the fire pit where he was pouring himself another cup of coffee. "What do you have, Mister Baker?" he asked as he strode toward his new gun bearer.

"Look here, sir." He pointed at the ground.

Roosevelt knelt down on one knee beside Baker. "Great guns! Puma tracks...I'd say a male, judging by how big it is." He got to his feet, backtracked the panther to where he entered the camp, turned and followed the prints in the damp, soft earth to his exit point. "Ha!"

"Looks like he just walked in while we were all asleep, paused for a few moments, turned, and then went back into the woods, sir," said Baker.

"A bold move, Reginald, no question about it...A bold move, indeed," said Roosevelt with a smile, nodding.

Middens rolled out of his soogan and also walked over, scratched his scraggly beard, as he too looked at the tracks. "Huh…Never seen the like, no sir, never seen the like…Panther walkin' into camp…Looks like the critter even sat down fer a spell…Could weigh meby two hunderd an' forty or fifty pounds."

Agent Thomas stepped back and searched the woods with his eyes. "That's amazing."

"Wonder why Snake ain't come back?" asked Tenkiller.

"Musta got caught in that storm," said Marquis Rudabaugh.

"Or fell into the creek," added Little Dime.

"Well, somethin' musta happened to 'im… Reckon I'll just have to take over, then," said Ugly George, with some authority.

"Why you?" asked Tenkiller.

"Didn't see none of you other dimwits jumpin' up to handle it," replied McSween.

"What if Snake comes back?" asked Bull Weaver.

Ugly George glared at the outlaw. "Then he comes back."

BONE

"Awright...*Boss*. What do we do?" asked Little Dime.

"Uh...We...uh, wait till what's left of Roosevelt's group packs their traps an' moves on down the trail deeper into the Seven Devils...that's what," replied McSween. "Little Dime, why don't you slip over an' keep an eyeball on 'em?"

"Why, shore...Boss," he replied with undisguised sarcasm, got to his feet, picked up his Winchester, and moved off down the trail toward the hunting party.

"Gonna kill that little turd when this is over," mumbled Ugly George as he watched Little Dime disappear around a bend.

Bass also watched Little Dime until he was out of sight from the dark shadows underneath a copse of fragrant junipers—the tiny fall purple berries on the female trees were ripening.

He inched his way backwards until he could stand, turned and slipped off through the brush like a wraith, paralleling the game trail. His buckskins kept the prickly dead foliage under the trees from getting to his skin.

"Hey, Bill," said Bass as he stepped from behind a thick red oak next to the trail as Little Dime, aka, Marshal Brushy Bill Roberts, got nearer. "Out fer a little stroll?"

Bill jumped and even drew his Thunderer. "Damn, Bass, like to have scared me out of a year's growth." He reholstered his pistol.

Reeves chuckled. "In yer case, that would be a travesty...Could pass fer a teenager."

Roberts grinned. "Well, I've done that a time or two when I was a Pinkerton."

"I 'magine...Goin' to check on Mister Roosevelt?"

"Yep, the new boss, Ugly George McSween, is giving out orders." He chuckled. "Not only is he ugly as a burnt boot, but isn't the sharpest knife in the drawer." He took it on himself to take over when Snake Smith didn't come back...Your doings? Heard your .38-40."

"You could say," Bass said with a smile. "Bone took care of Boone Prescott on the other side, 'long with Jack an' Selden confiscatin' Tall Jim an' Evil Carl's boots, guns, an' horses...Sent 'em packin' barefoot, unarmed, an' shank's mare outta the Nations, they did."

"Who's Bone?"

"Tell you later."

Bill gave Bass a confused look, and then continued, "That leaves Ugly George, Haywood Tenkiller, and Marquis Rudabaugh...Then there's Tarlton Brewster and Tobacca Bob Buckley back down the trail," added Bill. "All I know about."

"Bone is sendin' Bodie back down the trail fer Brewster an' Bob...Gonna try to bring Brewster back in shackles...if'n he can."

"Well, may be time to make our move," said Bill.

Bass looked at the smaller man and grinned his big toothy smile. "Mind yer right...Wish Bone an' Fiona wuz over here."

"Ask and ye shall receive," came a deep voice from the dense brush.

Bill and Bass spun around to see Bone step out on the trail.

"Durn, Bone, you could be a Injun," exclaimed Bass.

"Could go duck hunting with a hoe, too," added Bill, his five feet, seven inches looking up at Bone's six feet, eight."

The big man just smiled at the little man. "Naw, usually use a rake." He looked at Bass. "That's why the Recon Marines I was in are such an elite fighting force…not to say anything about the super secret black-ops group, the Black Eagle Force, Loraine and I are part of…Their motto is, 'You didn't see us…This didn't happen…We weren't here'." He grinned. "Would fit you like a glove, if you were in my time."

Bill looked at Bone, frowned, and arched his eyebrows, and then asked, "Is Fiona here?"

"Sent her and Bodie into Bass' camp, thought I'd catch up to you fellows and see what the next step is."

"How'd you git over here, Bone? Water's still too high to ford," asked Bass.

"Roots on a big tall cottonwood at the edge of the creek washed out and that son of a gun fell smooth across to this side up the creek a ways…We just walked across…Had to leave our horses, though…None of them wanted to walk across on that two foot wide tree trunk…Get them later."

Loraine set a pot of water on a flat rock next to the fire to boil.

"Hope that's for coffee," came a voice from behind her.

She jumped and spun around, reaching for her Kimber. "Fiona! You scared me. How'd ya'll get here?"

"Crossed on a tree downed across the creek by the storm," said Bodie, as he followed Fiona into camp. "Water's goin' down purty quick, though...Kinda reminds me of the *Llano Estacado* in west Texas...flash floods and all...Up fast, down fast."

"What's the *Llano Estacado*?" asked Lucy as she got up from her bedroll and walked toward the fire.

"Means 'Staked Plain'...Back in the early days of the Spanish trail between San Antone and Santa Fe, they marked it with stakes on account of it all lookin' the same...So travelers wouldn't get lost," commented Doctor Ashalatubbi as he dropped an armload of deadfall next to the fire.

She nodded. "I know the area of which you speak. My mate, Garin, and I passed over it when we were trying to get our antigravity drive engines restarted…just before we crashed at Aurora," said Lucy.

"Where's Bone?" asked Flynn.

"Went to find Bass…wherever he is," answered Fiona.

"He's scouting the bad guys," replied Loraine, and then turned at a voice.

"Found Bill, headin' back to locate Roosevelt's group an' Bone found us," said Bass as he, Bone, and Bill slipped into camp from the narrow game trail.

"Don't think I know this lady either…besides man mountain here," said Bill.

"Well, now that we's all here, reckon we kin tell you their story…Not that you'll believe a word of it, though…Uh…how's about you tell it Doc, not sure I understands it all," offered Bass.

"All right, but I suggest you all take a seat, this may take a little while." Winchester got to his feet.

"I'll help," said Lucy.

"I think I'm going to need you, star queen." He looked at Selden and Jack. "You already know about Lucy of course, but as to Bone and Loraine…"

Forty-five minutes later, he and Lucy finished Bone
and Loraine's story, "…and that's about the gist of
it…as far as we know," said Doctor Ashalatubbi.

"You were right, Bass, not sure I believe it, but
there they sit…Ain't never seen nothin' like their
shooters," commented Jack.

"And nobody knows exactly why they're here?"
asked Selden.

Bone and Loraine exchanged glances and both
shrugged.

"One, Bone saved Fiona's life by taking a bullet
for her," added Lucy. "As I said, I think they're here
as a matter of fate…meaning the Holy Entity, the
one God of us all, sent them. But, they're still here,
so that gives me pause to think there is something
they have to take care of yet."

"As a matter of ancient Indian philosophy, 'If
you travel to the past, then you are part of the
past…and always have been'," said *Anompoli Lawa*
as he looked at Bone and Loraine.

"Ooh, that's deep," commented Loraine.

"But, makes sense," added Bone.

"Makes my head hurt."

"I can help, Jack. Take your hat off," said Lucy as she walked over and put her hands on either side of his head.

A soft blue glow emanated from under her palms, and then disappeared. She held her hands in place for a moment, and then removed them. "Better?"

"Dangnation," he replied. "Thanks, Lucy."

"Well, all that notwithstanding, what's the plan?" asked Bodie.

"Well, I thinks we oughta surround 'em an' give 'em a chance to give theyselves up," suggested Bass.

"And if they don't want to play that game?" asked Loraine.

"I'd say that's up to them, Pard. Don't see that we have much choice but to take them out."

"I agree, Bone," said Fiona.

"An' a damned short time to think about it. The longer you give 'em…the more they think they kin beat you," commented Jack.

"Truer words were never spoken," added Selden.

"Well, we're all agreed. Now, the question is when do we go?" asked Sheriff Flynn.

"They're waitin' on me to get back with the information on the hunting party...Want to wait till they pack up an' move into the Seven Devils..."

Bass interrupted Bill with a look of concern on his face. "Where the woods be thicker...Gonna make it harder on us, too, I mind."

§§§

CHAPTER TWENTY-THREE

SEVEN DEVIL HILLS

Bone sat on a log, working on his second cup of coffee, studying Brushy Bill sitting on the other side of the fire. Finally he said, "You know, Marshal Roberts, I've made a study of what we call in our time, 'the old west', and especially William Bonney, aka Billy the Kid...There are several photographs of him, including a well-known ferrotype taken in 1879 or '80…Gotta tell you…You are the spitting image of the Kid."

Bill looked up from his own cup with a wry grin. "You don't say?"

"I do. Plus you've got his known attributes of height and weight…with small hands and large wrists."

Bill took another sip of his coffee. "The detective in you rising to the surface, Mister Bone?"

"Could say that." Bone frowned and then raised his right eyebrow. "William H. Bonney, Jr., aka Henry Antrim, aka Henry McCarty, aka…Ollie L. Roberts…Brushy Bill Roberts?"

Fiona and Sheriff Flynn glanced sharply at Bone and then at each other.

"Well, the papers said he was killed by Sheriff Pat Garrett in '81…If not, the Kid is still a wanted man with a price on his head," said Bill. "And I suspect that Big Casino would be a mite miffed if it was found out the man he shot that night at the Maxwell ranch…was not the Kid."

Bone looked at the small man, smiled and nodded. "That's what they say…also said Governor

Wallace pardoned every one of the Regulators…except for the Kid."

"That's true," commented Bill.

Bone grinned. "Well, you couldn't be him, anyway, you're a Deputy United States Marshal and weren't you a Pinkerton detective and a railroad detective?"

"I am and I was."

"Well, doesn't sound like William Bonney to me."

"Maybe the Kid was a victim of circumstance?" said Bill, and then took another sip of his coffee.

Bill watched as the hunting party moved out down the trail to the northeast, single file, deeper into the wilderness. Possum Middens led the procession that was smaller by three men than when they started.

Roosevelt and the Secret Service agent, Wesley Thomas, both carried their Winchesters across the bows of their saddles. The two remaining assistants' heads were on swivels as they constantly strained to see into the thick, dark, foreboding woods, apprehensive of what might be lurking there.

Bill turned, moved through the brush and headed deeper himself into the hills, paralleling the track of the hunting group.

The normal woods sounds of birds, crickets, cicadas and chattering squirrels weren't disturbed. The still damp forest floor from yesterday's rain made his passage silent.

Thirty minutes later, Brushy Bill entered Bass' camp to inform them of the movement, and then headed on back to his own camp to tell the outlaws Roosevelt's party had moved out.

"Well?" Ugly George asked as Bill walked in to the outlaw's camp and knelt down at the fire to pour himself some coffee fifteen minutes after leaving the marshal's location.

"Well?" George said louder.

When Bill finished filling his cup, he got to his feet and looked over at the new boss.

"Don't get your longjohns in a wad, McSween. Been on the trail through the woods getting back here for mor'n a hour." He took a sip from the cup.

"Dammit, Little Dime, don't pull that crap on me." His hand moved to the butt of his Colt.

Bill looked up and stared at him with his clear blue eyes and calmly said with no emotion, "Touch that shooter, McSween, an' that'll be the last mistake you'll ever make in this life." He took another sip. His steely gaze never wavered from the man.

Ugly George's face blanched as he quickly moved the right hand up to his nose, wiped across it with the back of his knuckles, cleared his throat and glanced around at the others. "Well…jest wanted to know is all," he said with no small amount of contrition.

Bill stared at George for a moment longer, making him even more nervous, before he finally spoke, "They're packin' up. Probably already on the trail by now…I expect they're going to camp at the headwaters of Gates Creek up the trail."

"Then that's where we'll hit 'em. The woods is too thick 'tween here an' there fer any easy shootin'," said Ugly George.

Bill looked at him and nodded. *Glad you picked that spot. Makes it better and safer for Bass and them.*

"That's the first thing you've said that makes sense, McSween," added Bull Weaver.

"We'll camp here," said Possum Middens, when Roosevelt's group entered a small clearing.

A spring bubbled out of some limestone rocks at the side of the hill on the west side of the glade, making a large clear pool at the bottom, and then flowed off and formed Gates Creek.

Teddy nodded. "Good choice, Middens. Fresh water and plenty of grass for the animals...Bully."

The gun bearer, Reginald Baker led his horse over to the stream overflowing out of the pool at the base of the cliff and let him drink. He noticed a plethora of tracks around the pool and stream.

He led his horse back to the group so he could strip the tack. "Mister Roosevelt, this is a good spot. I saw a lot of deer, elk...and bear tracks over at the pond, sir. Looks like the bear could be around three hundred pounds."

"A boar...Good," said Teddy. "Don't want to shoot a female. She might have cubs from last year or pregnant for this year...Any cat tracks?"

"Not that I can see, sir. But, the area's pretty well trampled...lot of tracks on top of each other...Could be."

"Bully, Mister Baker, bully...Soon as we strip the animals and grain them, you and I will see if we can get some camp meat...What say you?"

"I'll be ready, sir...We may not have to go far."

"Interesting, I'm..."

"I kin go git the camp meat, Mister Roosevelt...Know this country well," said Possum.

"Oh, I think not, Mister Middens. I enjoy the sport of hunting...Especially when it's for the table," replied Roosevelt.

"Whatever you want, sir...Wuz jest offerin'," Middens grumbled.

Roosevelt and Baker headed further to the northeast, rather than back toward the way they had come.

"Best to go this way, Mister Baker. Might have frightened any game animals back downstream with our passage…The deer will be more calm and probably feeding on acorns, pecans and hickory nuts this time of year."

"Very good, sir," the young man replied.

Roosevelt glanced around at the woods. "Very much like the Great Smokies. Ever hunted in the Great Smoky Mountains in Tennessee, Mister Baker?"

"Can't say as I have, sir." Reginald glanced up ahead, held up his hand, stopped and turned to his boss, and whispered, "Sir, look up ahead through those trees…a buck…Whitetail."

"Excellent eyesight, Mister Baker, how many points?"

Roosevelt and Baker both squatted down.

"I make it ten, sir."

"Let's move a little closer, so I can see better. Eyesight is not as good as it was when I was younger…a lot younger. Glad I have a scope on this rifle, don't shoot as well as I used to."

"Yessir."

They both rose and using a thick copse of wild plums for cover, they crept to within thirty yards of the feeding buck.

Roosevelt slowly dropped to one knee and brought his .45-90 Winchester to his shoulder and sighted in on the deer. He squeezed the trigger and the big bore Winchester kicked against his shoulder, but he gave it scant notice.

Initially, the large gray-white cloud of gunsmoke obscured their vision. When the evening breeze cleared the air, Roosevelt looked to where he had shot.

"Well, I apparently missed, Mister Baker...he's gone."

Reginald peered closer. "No, sir. He dropped where he stood. I can see one side of his rack sticking up through the grass...Your shot must have cut his spine."

"Bully! Let's go field dress him and then carry him back to camp. We'll have venison tonight."

Everyone's head snapped around to the northeast at the report of the shot that echoed down the valley.

"Big bore. Probably a .45-90...I'd say somebody's hunting for camp meat," said Bone.

"I mind yer right, big man. Wesley said that's what Roosevelt brung with him fer huntin'. Said

Winchester custom made 'im a 1886 model...engraved an' all...He also had a '76, .45-75, they made fer 'im, too," commented Bass.

"Must have gotten a hit, only heard one shot," said Bodie.

"I'd say they're havin' venison steaks tonight," added Flynn. "Too bad we gotta have a cold camp since we're close enough they could see our fire."

"We'll have to get by on jerky and those hot water cornbread dodgers Loraine made last night," said Fiona. "We have some canned pickled-peaches, too."

"Well, hey, that saves the day. Love me some pickled-peaches...yum."

"Bone, you'd eat anything that wasn't tied down or still walking," quipped Loraine. "Those tins of sardines and hogs head cheese you brought along when we went fishing and transported here was enough to gag a maggot."

"Beats going without, Pard," he replied. "Don't look like you been starving much." He glanced at her rear end.

"Damn you, Bone, I'm going to kill you," she retorted as she picked up a stick from the deadfall pile at the fire pit and threw it at him.

He ducked and grinned at her.

"By the Lord Harry…Do ya'll go on this way all the time?" asked Jack.

Bone and Loraine exchanged glances and both nodded.

"Huh…Just as well be married," he muttered.

Bone and Loraine simultaneously replied. "Oh, God, Jack…We'd kill each other in a week."

Lucy covered her mouth with her hand and giggled at the pair, and then all but she jumped as the piercing woman-like scream of a panther reverberated along the creek from close by in the woods…

§§§

CHAPTER TWENTY-FOUR

KIAMICHI WILDERNESS

The sun's rays created a golden glow at the skyline as it approached the eastern horizon from its night time lair, turning the deep purple sky to a dark blue graduating to a lighter blue closer to the heavily forested hills and the great yellow orb just below the skyline.

Ugly George's gang were gathered on the south side of Roosevelt's camp. McSween had given instructions to the men on whom to shoot, being careful not to hit the Assistant Secretary, Middens and one other.

Teddy was ensconced in an army style tent on the west side of the glade. The others were scattered about around the firepit in their soogans.

The entire camp was still asleep save for Mark Putnam, one of the surviving assistants, who was stoking the coals and adding fresh deadfall so he could put on the Arbuckles to boil.

He picked up the pot and headed toward the stream to fill it when a shot rang out and he dropped in mid-stride. A ball of white gunsmoke curled out of the bushes on the southwest side of the clearing.

The outlaws stepped out of the brush, firing at the bedrolls.

Baker and the other assistant, Cletus Simpson, startled out of their deep slumber, jumped up only to take a round each and slump back on their blankets.

Middens and Thomas raised up grabbed their guns and then dived back to the ground as bullets whistled about.

BONE

Jack McGann walked out of a clump of cedars on the north edge of the clearing and fired both barrels of a ten gauge coach gun into the air.

"You boys hold yer shootin'…Bass Reeves Deputy US Marshal. Yer surrounded. Suggest you give yerselves up er suffer yer death," Bass' deep voice boomed as he stepped from behind a large hickory tree.

"Go to hell," shouted Haywood Tenkiller. "Ain't nobody out there but you two.

Bone, Flynn, Fiona, and Selden all materialized from the woods on three sides of the glen to join Bass and Jack.

"Wrong, asswipe," said Bone as he pointed his .50 cal at Tenkiller.

The Choctaw halfbreed swung his cocked Colt in Bone's direction. He was blasted to his back before he could even pull the trigger as the big 500 S&W roared like a cannon when the big man fired.

Roosevelt burst out of his tent with his .38 Long Colt Army revolver in his hand.

"Get down, Mister Roosevelt," shouted Sheriff Flynn, the nearest on that side to him.

Teddy quickly did as he was told and flattened himself to the ground.

Ugly George McSween, Marquis Rudabaugh and Bull Weaver all opened fire at the officers.

Fiona quickly took out Weaver with two shots from her .38-40 matched Colts. Both impacted his chest not a half inch apart.

Rudabaugh tried to take cover while shooting at Bass and Selden. Lindsey took a round and dropped to a knee as he, Bass and Flynn all fired at the outlaw—they each scored. Marquis Rudabaugh's bullet riddled body was flung backward like a rag doll by the fusillade of lead.

Bill turned to McSween and holstered his Colt Thunderer. "All right George, now's your chance. I'm Deputy US Marshal Bill Roberts…Make your play."

Ugly George wheeled to his right. "You lousy traitor. Might have known." He thumbed the hammer on the single-action Colt in his hand, but, never got the chance to pull the trigger as Bill drew, fired and fanned two more shots into McSween as he was falling to the dirt.

"Jesus, Mary and Joseph," Bone muttered at the speed of Bill's action.

Abruptly, the silence was deafening. Heavy clouds of the noxious gunsmoke hung in the air.

Roosevelt looked up, and then got up and holstered his .38. "Excellent work men...uh, people," he corrected himself as he noticed Fiona. "Excellent...Bully."

Middens and Thomas also got to their feet and made their way over to Roosevelt. Each still had a pistol in their hands.

Possum Middens unexpectedly threw his left arm about Roosevelt's neck, pulled the stocky man to him and held his Remington .44 against his side. "Ain't over, lawdogs," he hissed.

A hole suddenly appeared between his eyes as a Colt roared. His eyes rolled back in his head as a tiny rivulet of blood ran down the side of his nose just before he collapsed to the ground like a wet paper bag.

"My God," exclaimed Roosevelt as he looked over at Fiona, the gunsmoke cloud still in front of her.

"No it's not," said Wesley as he stepped behind Roosevelt with his S&W Russian in his back.

"Thomas, what is this?" asked Bass.

"Insurance, Reeves, insurance..." answered the agent. "I never trusted Middens and his bunch to get this done."

"Why?" asked Jack. "You've been a good agent, Wesley."

"Money, of course, Marshal…Lots of money." He looked over at Fiona and grinned. He was a little shorter than Roosevelt. "I'm not dumb enough to expose myself to one of your Colts, Marshal…Now, I suggest you drop them."

She glared at the agent and dropped both her Colts to the ground.

Bodie and Loraine stepped into Tarlton and Tobaccca Bob's camp. The two men were already up and Brewster was setting the pot on a flat rock close to the fire to boil.

Bob was out of sight in the bushes on the other side of camp, relieving himself.

"I like mine strong," said Bodie as he drew his .45 and pointed at the straw boss.

The man looked up. "Huh?" His eyes darted from the muzzle of Bodie's gun to Loraine with her Kimber in her hand held out at arm's length.

"Texas Ranger. You're under arrest, friend," added Bodie.

BONE

"What?...Hey, this ain't Texas," Brewster said belligerently as he got to his feet.

"That's all right, he can't read a map anyway." Loraine nodded at Bodie.

A shot rang out from the bushes, Bodie spun around and fell to his knees, and then on down to the ground. Five rapid shots, that sounded like one continuous roar, from Loraine's semiautomatic .45, followed as an instant answer.

The bushes were flattened by Tobacca Bob's body as he collapsed on top of them. There were five exit holes in his back that could fit inside a pickle jar lid.

Brewster eased his .44 from his holster slowly with two fingers and dropped it to the ground, and then raised both hands over his head and knelt down beside the firepit. "Don't shoot me, please for God's sake, don't shoot me."

"God has nothing to do with it, scumbag," replied Loraine.

Bodie groaned, rolled over and handed her his shackles. "Here," he whispered in pain.

She pushed the skinny man to his face, holstered her Kimber .45 pulled his arms behind him and snapped the cuffs about his wrists, none too gently.

"Now stay put or I'll have to hurt you," she said as she knelt beside Bodie and pulled his coat back.

There was a circle of blood forming on his side just above the hip. Loraine ripped the shirt back to see a shallow five inch groove across his right love handle.

"You'll live." She pulled a handkerchief from her beaded buckskin possibles bag, that matched her buckskin top and pants, slung over her shoulder and pressed it against his side.

"Annabel's gonna kill me...Said not to come home with holes in me."

"Not a hole...More of a shallow gash, really. Can you walk?" she asked as the sound of gunfire came from the direction of the hunting camp. It stopped momentarily as they heard a ten gauge shotgun. Then the .44 and .45 cal pistol shots continued, but were separated by the louder report from a .50 caliber.

Thomas' head exploded in a cloud of red mist, covering Teddy Roosevelt with brain matter, bone parts and blood as the rogue Secret Service agent dropped to the ground like a rotten apple falling from the tree. Roosevelt had instinctively ducked at the tremendous explosion from his right.

All the others looked over at Bone, standing at the far side on the clearing to the side, twenty yards away. He was still holding his 500 with a two-handed grip at arm's length, pointed to just behind Roosevelt where Thomas had been standing. A grin spread across his face.

Teddy staggered forward a step and dropped to his knees, wiping the gray bloody corruption from his head.

The final single shot was from the .50 caliber again and much louder than the others.

"Bone…That finished it," Loraine said.

Bodie looked off in the direction of Roosevelt's camp and then at her. "What was that…a cannon?" he asked.

"No, just Bone's handgun," she commented nonchalantly.

"Jesus and all his disciples," he muttered as he got to his feet holding the pad against his side.

Loraine grabbed Brewster's elbow, helped him to his feet, and led him toward the game trail in the direction of Roosevelt's camp. Bodie hobbled along behind them.

Jack was the nearest and ran over to the politician. "Are you awright, sir?" he asked as he started helping him to his feet.

"Yes, yes, but incredible shots, just incredible…especially the one from the big man…What the hell kind of gun is that?" Roosevelt asked Bone as he picked up his Pince nez glasses that had fallen from his nose.

Jack was joined by Bass, Sheriff Flynn and Fiona while Selden limped over.

"Uh, it's an experimental from Smith & Wesson…A .50 caliber," replied Bone.

".50 caliber handgun? My God in Heaven," he responded.

"You hit in the leg, Selden?" asked Bass.

"Yeah…through and through. Didn't get the artery…least don't think so," he answered with a grimace. "Burns like fire, though."

"Here, lay down," said Fiona as she grabbed a blanket from one of the bedrolls and threw it behind him.

Bone walked over and handed her his Bowie. She quickly split his pant leg with the razor sharp blade to expose the wound. "Thanks, Bone. Somebody get me something to clean this with and something to wrap it," Fiona directed.

"There are some towels in my tent, Marshal," Roosevelt said. "Bring me one, too. Like to clean that would-be assassin's blood and gore off." He slung a chunk of Thomas' skull from the back of his neck.

"Don't think theys gonna assassinate you, sir. Least not yet...Think they's gonna hold you fer ransom of some sort," commented Bass.

Selden opened a black leather pouch attached to his gunbelt and handed Fiona a vial of white powder.

"What's this?" she asked.

"Powdered alum, it'll help stop the bleedin'," he replied.

"Wonderful stuff." She pulled the cork from the bottle just as Flynn returned with several towels. "Thanks, dear."

Fiona took one, ripped it in two and started wiping the blood from the front and back of Selden's leg. Then she sprinkled some of the powder on both holes and tore two strips from the other half of the towel and folded them into pads for each hole. "Hold these in place, Mason, while I wrap the leg…Goodness, they've almost stopped bleeding." She tied off the end of the wrapping. "That should hold till we get you to Doctor Ashalatubbi and Lucy back at camp."

"Yep, that's good stuff, I'm never without it…Not in our business," Selden grunted.

Bass looked up to see Loraine leading Brewster by the arm followed by a limping Bodie.

"Where you hit Ranger?" he asked.

"Graze to my side. Just above the one I got down to Red River Station that time…The barkeep there poured some tequila on it…Hurt worse than the bullet wound."

"I have some liquor in my tent, son. Not tequila, but some good sour mash," offered Roosevelt. "Wouldn't hurt to soak Marshal Lindsey's leg wounds either."

"Oh, joy," said Bodie and Selden together.

§§§

CHAPTER TWENTY-FIVE

KIAMICHI WILDERNESS

"Guess we got some buryin' to do for them bodies start a stinkin'. Reckon we oughta send somebody back to camp to git Doc Ashalatubbi and Lucy, an' then bring the horses over here," said Jack.

"That won't be necessary, nephew," came a voice from the edge of camp where the trail entered.

They all looked up to see Winchester riding in on his horse with Lucy sitting behind him, her arms wrapped around his ample waist.

"Lucy knew when the fight was over, she reads Bone like a book, and suggested we head this way. Said I had some words to say over some departed souls," he said.

Winchester Ashalatubbi was not only a trained physician, the tribal Shaman, but was also had a degree in divinity. In other words, he could birth you, heal your body and spirit and bury you.

"But, a couple of you will need to go back to camp and bring the horses, Fiona's mule, Spot, and our supplies...I'm assuming we'll be moving camp to here."

Lucy slipped from the back of the horse and ran directly to Selden who was still lying on the blanket.

"Fiona, help me, please," she said.

They knelt down beside Selden and placed their hands on either side of his leg above the wound.

They both closed their eyes in deep concentration. In a moment, a soft blue glow emanated from their palms. The glow from Lucy's hands was brighter than Fiona's.

The two women held their position for about three minutes, and then the glow slowly diffused into Selden's body. They removed their hands and sat back on their knees, heads on their chests and took deep breaths.

After a bit, they slowly rose shakily to their feet.

"May I have some water?" asked Lucy.

"Me too," added Fiona.

Bone brought them each a canteen of water from the spring and they drank heavily until they were satisfied.

Fiona stepped around Selden's legs and hugged the little woman.

Selden raised up on his elbows, reached down and felt his leg. He undid the wrapping to see that what was left of the wounds was a slightly depressed red area. It had healed.

He looked up at the two women, smiled, nodded and got to his feet. "I'll be darned."

"What the hell did I just witness," asked a stunned Roosevelt.

"I suppose we have some explaining to do," said Doctor Ashalatubbi.

"Just a moment, *Anompoli Lawa*," said Lucy as she stepped over to Bodie who had been watching the proceeding.

She placed both her tiny hands on his side over his wound. The same thing occurred. In a moment, she removed her hands and stepped back as Bodie unwrapped his bandages. His graze also had healed.

"I need to sit down, now," commented Lucy.

"As do I," said Fiona. "That is so draining."

Doctor Ashalatubbi turned to Teddy Roosevelt. "Sir, if you'll have a seat next to the ladies, we'll fill you in on Lucy, Bone and Loraine with the understanding that it must remain here."

Roosevelt nodded and sat down on a log next to Lucy.

"First off, Lucy is not who you think…"

An hour later, Winchester finished debriefing Theodore Roosevelt. "And that's pretty much it, sir. There is much even I don't understand…especially how Lucy's people mode of travel works or why Bone and Loraine are here."

Roosevelt got to his feet and paced back and forth a few moments in deep thought. Finally he stopped and looked at the Shaman. "I don't think you have anything to worry about, *Anompoli Lawa*, I doubt anyone would believe me if I did tell them...Aliens from another world...Time travelers...Sounds like something from a Jules Verne or H. G. Wells novel."

"I agree, both gentlemen are referred to as scientific and social prophets, too." said Fiona.

"Much of what they wrote about in their science fiction novels will come to pass," said Bone.

"Speaking of which, I would love to ask Bone and Loraine some questions, though."

Bone and Loraine looked at each other and then at Doctor Ashalatubbi.

"I have an idea of what those questions are, sir, but according to Lucy and the good doctor, it wouldn't be ethical for us to answer questions about the future." He glanced at Lucy again. "The future has already happened and it has to play out that way...The only thing I will say is it's already been in the papers that you're planing on resigning and joining the Army for the coming conflict with Spain..."

"We suggest..." Loraine glanced at Bone. "...that you call your outfit the Rough Riders..."

Bone picked up "…and that you should run for the presidency in two years."

Bone added, "Your foreign policy should be 'Speak softly and carry a big stick'.

Roosevelt sat down heavily on the log back next to Lucy and took a deep breath. "Well, I don't know what to say." He looked up at Bone and Loraine. "I don't suppose you will tell me if I'm successful?"

"No, sir, I won't," Bone replied.

"Well, all right then, bully…I shot a deer yesterday, I think we should have some grilled venison for breakfast. What say you?" He glanced around the gathered assemblage.

"I could eat a bear," said Bone.

Roosevelt grinned the famous smile he was known for. "Maybe tomorrow…That deer is hanging from that big pecan tree over…It's gone!"

He got to his feet and pointed. "It was right there when we went to bed last night, drained, gutted and skinned. We had steaks and grilled heart for supper…What in blue blazes?"

They walked over to where the buck had been hung to cool. Jack looked at the frayed end of the rope it was hung with, then knelt down and studied the ground.

"I'll be go to hell," he said, and then looked up at Bone. "Well, biggun, you may get your wish about could eat a bear. That's exactly what took Mister Roosevelt's deer...Not goin' to take it very far, I'll wager. He'll hide it in the woods...cover it with leaves an' branches an' feed on it fer a week. The riper it gits, the better...Be easy to find, right Bass?"

"I mind yer right, Jack."

"I say let's have some of Jack's famous beans an' bacon for breakfast, then," commented Bodie.

"Sure you don't want bacon an' beans?" Jack grinned.

"After we take care of the deceased," said Winchester.

"Oh, yeah, speaking of gettin' ripe...Good idea," added Sheriff Flynn.

It was midmorning by the time they had buried everyone, and then had a late breakfast. The outlaws were placed in a common grave, but Reginald Baker, Mark Putnam and Cletus Simpson were buried in individual graves covered with stones from the creek. The Shaman had read from the Bible over each grave.

"I think it's time to go hunting," said Roosevelt.

"I'd like to go with you, sir," commented Bone.

"Of course."

"I'll go an' track 'im fer you…You don't mind," added Bass.

"I'd be honored, Marshal Reeves…Shall we go then, gentlemen?"

"He's talking to you, too, Bone," snipped Loraine.

"Wait'll I get back, Pard."

Bone and Bass got to their feet, pitched what was left of their coffee on the ground and set their cups nearby for use when they returned.

Bass led out from the starting point, which was the pecan tree where the buck was hung.

"Trackin' be easy to start with. See where he drug the carcass through the leaves…Cain't believe ya'll didn't hear nothin'," commented Bass as he pointed out the disturbed leaves on the forest floor.

"He's definitely a big one all right," said Bone.

"Tops 300 hunderd pounds, I wager," agreed Bass.

"This will stop him." Roosevelt held up his .45-90 caliber Winchester.

"Still best to make a head shot, sir. They're mighty tenacious animals. They'll keep a goin' even when they be already dead...but don't know it yet."

"That's when hunters get themselves killed," added Bone.

"Here's his stash, right next to that game trail. Makes it easy fer him to git back to." Bass pointed out a mound of leaves and branches and the hoof sticking out one side.

"Looks like he's heading to water, doesn't it, Bass?"

"I'd say, Bone...He may be layin' up takin' a little nap after eatin' his fill an' storin' his cache," said Bass. "Real fresh tracks, too...Meby a hour or less."

"Spent most of the morning eating...I betcha," added Bone.

They rounded a bend in the trail along the edge of the creek with trees on one side and boulders on the other. The big bruin was curled up asleep under a huge white oak.

"Look!" exclaimed Roosevelt.

Bone and Bass both turned to him with their fingers to their lips for quiet. Too late.

The startled huge black bear lunged to his feet and looked around to find whatever had the temerity to disturb his sleep. He spotted the three men just down the trail, roared his displeasure and charged.

Roosevelt quickly levered a shell in the chamber of his Winchester calmly put it to his shoulder and squeezed the trigger at the monster animal bearing down on them.

Click. A dud.

"Damn," he exclaimed and hurriedly jacked the lever on the rifle for another shell—it jammed.

Bone already had his 500 in his hand. He raised it for a two-handed head shot as the giant bear was less than fifteen feet away charging at them at thirty miles an hour—less than a half-second for a kill shot...

§§§

CHAPTER TWENTY-SIX

KIAMICHI WILDERNESS CAMP

Fiona and Lucy had lain down for a nap inside Roosevelt's tent from their exhaustive healing ministrations to Marshal Lindsey and Ranger Hickman.

Jack, Bodie, Selden, and Sheriff Flynn walked back to their camp to get their horses, Fiona's mule, Spot, and the camp supplies.

"Hows that leg, Selden?" asked Flynn.

"It's a bit sore and tight, Sheriff, but this walk done it some good."

"Hey, look, somethin' got into our food packs," exclaimed Bodie.

"Musta been another bear. If there's food, the dang scudders will find it. They'll eat anything," said Jack.

"Be damned...Look at this." Flynn pointed at the tracks around the torn open poke sacks and saddlebags.

"Well, well...Boys, that ain't no bear," said Jack as he looked back up at Flynn, Selden and Bodie.

"What is it?" asked Bodie.

"Lofa, as the Injuns call it...The wild man of the forest," Jack said as he got to his feet. "Damn, hope the animals is all right...Say, where's Newton? Tol' him to stay here."

They started looking around through the bushes.

"Jack, why don't you go check on the horses," said Flynn.

BONE

"Good idee." Jack headed down the trail toward the small clearing where they had picketed the stock.

He walked into the clearing, looked around, turned and yelled back up the trail. "Hey, fellers, down here."

Fiona and Lucy sat up at about the same time and looked at each other.

"Well, I feel better, don't you?" asked Fiona.

"Very rejuvenated, yes."

"Like some coffee?"

"Love some," replied Lucy.

They got to their knees and crawled out the flap of the small tent, stood up and stretched.

"The boys should be back soon...Is there any coffee," Fiona asked Bill, sitting next to the fire with Roosevelt.

He glanced over at the ladies and grinned. "Just made a fresh pot."

"Oh, good," said Lucy. She looked up as Jack and the others led the mounts into camp with Newton trotting alongside.

"Gonna take these boys down and picket 'em out with the others, be back in a few...Newton wants to say howdy," said Jack.

The red and white Border Collie bounded over to Fiona, raised up, put his paws on her hips, and pressed the top of his head against her stomach. His form of a hug.

Fiona knelt down and rubbed behind both of the loyal dog's ears. He flopped over on his back.

"Oh, want the belly rub, huh?"

She started rubbing his stomach as Jack, Selden, Bodie and her husband walked back into camp with their soogans, saddlebags and what was left of the food pokes.

"Where's the rest of the food?" asked Fiona.

Before Bone could pull the trigger on his hand-cannon, a tawny blur launched from the top of the boulder alongside the trail. A two hundred and fifty pound mountain lion slammed into the bear just as he raised up to swat Theodore Roosevelt into the next world.

BONE

The bear turned his attention to the flashing claws of the puma. The big cat dodged and leapt up on the back of the boar, biting him behind the neck.

Roosevelt, Bone and Bass backed away from the gargantuan battle being fought between the two rulers of the forest. They watched in rapt awe at the two giant predators in their fight to the death.

The two animals rolled over and over. The bear tried to get the clinging catamount off his back. He finally succeeded, stood and swatted the cat head over heels ten feet away.

The big puma jumped to his feet and launched from where he landed to collide with the bear. They wrapped their paws around each other like a pair of lovers. The cat brought his hind feet up, grabbed the bear under the throat with his jaws and ripped down the animal's stomach with the razor sharp claws on his back feet.

The bruin roared in his pain and pawed at the big cat attached to his throat. His struggles grew less and less as his nemesis crunched down on his windpipe and juggler vein. He staggered and fell forward, but the panther leapt free to keep from being pinned under the three hundred pound behemoth.

The bloodied mountain lion turned his massive head, looked at Bone, Bass and Roosevelt, and hissed.

Bone slowly raised his .50 caliber handgun toward the feline again, but was interrupted by a coughing bark from the side of the trail. The big cat and the men turned their heads to the sound.

An eight foot tall, hairy, manlike creature stood at the edge of the trail upright, on two feet.

"Lofa," whispered Bass.

The creature grunted, looked at the three men with his golden eyes, coughed again, turned and walked back into the woods. The panther hissed once more at the men and left, padding alongside the Sasquatch. They were soon swallowed up by the dark forest.

Bone, Roosevelt and Bass exchanged glances.

Lucy jumped up from where she was sitting next to the fire and looked off in the direction Bone, Bass and Roosevelt had taken.

"What is it, Lucy?" asked Fiona.

BONE

She looked back at the other woman and then at the rest of the group gathered around the fire having coffee.

"I think I'll let them tell you. I believe some of you need to go help them with the bear...Just take the game trail," Lucy said.

"I didn't hear no shot," commented Jack. "Would have heard that big bore son of a gun of Mister Roosevelt's or Bone's .50 cal...if they were fired anywhere in this valley, that's for sure an' for certain."

"No matter, I think you should go," said Lucy.

Jack, Bodie and Flynn, set their cups down, got to their feet and headed toward the trail.

"Come on Newton, you can go," said Flynn.

The faithful dog spun around twice and darted toward the game trail ahead of the men.

"Better take some rope," commented Bill.

"Why, ain't you comin'?" asked Jack.

"All right, I just have some pondering to do...guess I can do that when we get back...I'll get a rope and be right behind you."

"Don't put yerself out none, now," quipped Jack.

295

They approached Bass, Bone and Roosevelt in the middle of the trail. The three had already skinned the bear and were in the process of removing the best cuts of meat and placing them on the still warm skin, along with the head, lying beside the carcass.

Newton stopped, growled and walked stiff legged with the hair along his back raised up toward the bear.

"He's already dead, son," said Flynn as he reached down and rubbed Newton's head.

The hair on his back went down, he looked up at his chosen master and wagged his tail.

"How'd you kill it? I didn't hear no shot," said Jack.

"Don't think you're going to believe it, Jack," replied Bone.

"Try me. Been around you an' Lucy long enough, I'll believe most anything."

As they finished removing the choice cuts and sweetmeats from the bear and giving Newton his share, the three men told Jack and the others what happened...

BONE

Jack wrapped the rope around the hide filled with the prime pieces while Bass made a small travois for the bear meat that Bone volunteered to drag the short distance back to camp.

"Yer right big man, ain't sure I believe it," said Jack.

"Gotta admit Jack, proof's in the puddin', said Bodie.

"Point." Jack looked around at the dark woods.

"He's gone, Jack...Him *and* his cat," said Roosevelt.

"Guess I shoulda come along with you boys," said Jack.

"If wishes and wants were wings, Jack, a frog wouldn't bump his ass every time he hopped," offered Bill.

"Nine-tenths of wisdom is being wise in time," said Teddy with his grin.

Bone grinned and glanced at the future president of the United States.

Back at camp, they filled the girls in on what happened.

"I will have to say this is the most interesting hunting trip I've ever been on...An Alien, time-travelers and a Sasquatch with a mountain lion for a companion...It's a shame. I won't be able to tell a soul." Roosevelt laughed and flashed his toothy smile. "For one thing I couldn't get elected dog catcher...The newspapers would all say I was loony, balmy...belong in the funny farm."

"Look at it this way, Mister Roosevelt, you'll have some great memories...and you'll know things very few people on this planet will ever know," said Bone with a grin. "At least, not in your lifetime."

§§§

EPILOGUE

MCGANN CABIN
ARBUCKLE MOUNTAINS

Bone and Loraine sat on the porch of Jack and Angie's cabin, north of Ardmore, in the Chickasaw Nation. Bass, Jack, Fiona, Sheriff Flynn, Lucy and Doctor Ashalatubbi also were on the big wraparound porch with cups of Angie's coffee, enjoying the morning.

The tumbling white water of Honey Creek could easily be heard up on the porch as it flowed away from seventy-seven foot tall Turner Falls.

"So, you found out who was behind that fiasco, did you, Marshal Reeves?" asked Mason Flynn.

Bass chuckled. "Yeah, we weren't gettin' 'ny information out of that Brewster feller till Bone here asked if'n he could talk to him...in private. Didn't see no harm in it an' be danged if'n it weren't ten minutes 'fore that skinny malefactor wuz singin' like a little birdie.

"We done know'd that his boss was Congressman Alexander Casserly of north Texas, been watchin' him...Well, an' it seems he had been paid a whole rafter of money by this Ambassador Don Miguel Fernández, of Spain...with more to come when the job was done."

"And I would surmise that he was under the direction of someone higher up?" added Fiona.

"Uh, huh, you could say...Casserly led the State Department direct to the Prime Minister of Spain, one Antonio Cánovas Del Castillo...War is a comin', folks."

"Seems that Spain was well aware that Theodore Roosevelt was the main hawk in Washington and was pushing the government to kick Spain out of Cuba and the Philippines, any way necessary...They figured to get some gold bullion for ransom and then they were going to kill Roosevelt and remove the primary impetus to the threat," said Bone.

"How did you get him to talk, Bone?" asked Doctor Ashalatubbi.

Bone shrugged and got a sly grin on his face. "Hey, didn't lay a finger on him...just told him about some of the things the al-Qaeda and the Taliban in Afghanistan would do to prisoners to get them to talk." He laughed. "After he threw up and wet his pants, couldn't shut him up."

Lucy grinned at the big man and nodded.

"Bone can be very persuasive. I've seen him interrogate suspects and perpetrators before," said Loraine.

"So, the government would not have paid the ransom?" asked Sheriff Flynn.

"Nope. They know'd better," answered Bass.

"It's the same in our time for kidnappers. We've found that even when the ransom is paid...the kidnappers will usually kill the victim anyway," added Loraine.

"It's like I said before, 'Follow the money,'…Time's are not going to change much in that regard," commented Bone.

"Did you say Bill was resigning his commission with the US Marshals Office?" asked Jack.

"That's what he said," replied Fiona.

"Knew he would when he found out Teddy was resigning from the administration and joining the Army for the potential war with Spain," commented Bone.

"What's he gonna do?" asked Bass.

Bone glanced at his partner. "He's going to join the Rough Riders that Roosevelt will be forming…He becomes a hero in the Spanish American war."

"We're goin' to war with Spain?" asked Flynn.

Bone nodded. "Like I said earlier, it was going to happen anyway…America's newest battleship, USS Maine, is going to go down to Cuba in a show of force in February of next year. She blows up and sinks in the harbor at Havana, killing a bunch of the crew. The United States thinks the ship hit a

Spanish mine and declared war…only lasts about a month."

"We won, I take it?" commented Jack.

Bone nodded. "Oh, yeah…Teddy becomes a big time hero with his Rough Riders in Cuba. Bill is going with him."

"He mentioned in the Kiamichis, he was pondering on something. He told me later that was it," said Fiona.

"Yeah…Funny thing is, USS Maine didn't hit a Spanish mine, she blew up on her own. The powder magazine was next to the coal bunker next to the boilers. Some coal dust caught fire and set off the munitions."

"So it was an accident?" asked Doctor Ashalatubbi.

"Yep, but the United States would have found a way to start the war anyhow…largely pushed by Roosevelt," answered Bone.

"What on earth for?" asked Fiona.

"Our government wanted Spain out of this hemisphere, Cuba and the Philippines…Cuba was just a little too close to our shores," responded Bone.

"Does ol' Teddy become president?" inquired Jack.

Bone grinned, glanced around at the others and took a sip of his coffee. He looked over at Doctor Ashalatubbi. "Doc, you mentioned you knew how we can get back to our time."

Anompoli Lawa took a sip of his own coffee. He was holding Jack and Angie's adopted daughter, Baby Sarah, in his lap. She was playing with his Chickasaw bone and bead necklace.

"As I mentioned before, the spiral petroglyphs at various locations…basically around the world, were placed there by our ancestors at the direction of a race of space travelers prior to the *Anunnaki*, Lucy's people. They were to indicate a recurring electromagnetic vortex, which acted as a portal in the space/time continuum."

"Oh, here we go again. Gonna git another headache."

"I'll fix it, Jack," said Lucy with a smile.

The Shaman also smiled and continued, "According to our legends, the star people used the vortexes as a gate or portal to travel to other worlds throughout the galaxy, dimensions, and time."

Jack put his fingers to the bridge of his nose between his eyes.

"We believe they had various ways of controlling it since it could do the things I mentioned...We are only aware of one," Ashalatubbi said.

"And that would be?" questioned Loraine.

He looked at Bone and Loraine. "Time travel...The locations are said to become active normally every blue moon...thats when we have two full moons in a month. Normally blue moons come only about every two or three years.

"Once in a blue moon...Wondered where that expression came from," commented Bone. "But, it wasn't a blue moon when we were transported here."

"That's true, Bone, but the *Anunnaki* believe the locations were chosen for their inherent base magnetism, much like the ley lines around the world. When the storm passed over you and lightning hit the hill where the cave was, it temporarily activated the vortex."

"But, why did we come to this particular time?" asked Loraine.

"As I said earlier, I think the Holy Entity sent the storm because it was time for you to be here," said Lucy. She glanced at the Shaman. "It's like *Anompoli Lawa* said, '...you are part of the past...and always have been."

"But, we always won't, because we exist in the twenty-first century, too," added Bone. "We will be going back."

"'Once in a blue moon...'" said Lucy with a twinkle in her eye.

Bone looked at Doctor Ashalatubbi. "So when's the next blue moon?"

"Not until next June 18."

Bone looked at Loraine. "Eight months...Well, Pard, guess we do what Theodore Roosevelt will say, 'Do what you can, with what you have, where you are'."

"However, I think you should tell Fiona and Mason one of the reasons you are here...with the other being saving Teddy Roosevelt's life for more important things besides hunting," suggested Lucy.

Bone pursed his lips, nodded, looked at Loraine, and then at Fiona and Mason Flynn. "Fiona, we apparently were sent here initially for me to save your life by taking that bullet meant for you."

She shook her head. "Why was that so important that I not die then...I don't understand."

Bone paused a long moment looking at them, and then grinned and said, "Because you and Mason are my great-grandparents...You're carrying my grandmother."

Fiona brought her hand to her mouth and her steel-gray eyes got big as saucers.

Mason's jaw dropped to his chest.

She finally nodded. "Oh, my...You're our great-grandson? My goodness. It all fits, now...and I'm carrying your grandmother? It's a girl, then."

"Uh, huh...Should I call you gran and gramps?"

Fiona and Mason looked at each other, then back at Bone, smiled, and said simultaneously, "Only if you want to get shot."

§§§§§

PREVIEW OF COMING
ATTRACTIONS

BONE'S LAW

BY

KEN FARMER

CHAPTER ONE

MONTAGUE COUNTY, TEXAS

Thirty-five year old Sheriff Brad Jamison reined his red roan gelding to the right of the wagon road they had been tracking along. He looked across the Red toward the little river town of Leon in the Chickasaw Nation.

He saw a puff of white smoke, and then it felt like someone had dropped an anvil on his chest.

He looked down at a dime-size hole where the second button on the gray striped shirt under a black vest used to be. What was there now was a red stain slowly spreading outward from the hole.

The sound of a big bore rifle echoed across the Red River valley.

"Oh, damn," he said as he slipped left sideways from the saddle and fell to the dusty road like a rag doll.

The roan horse shied to the right when the sheriff's body hit the ground, spun around and headed back toward the barn and safety at a gallop in Montague, the county seat of Montague County, Texas.

SKEENS BOARDING HOUSE
GAINESVILLE, TEXAS

Bone sat on the green settee in the parlor, scanning through the Gainesville Daily Register. His partner, Loraine Rodriguez was reading one of the owner, Faye Skeens novels, *The Picture of Dorian Gray*, by Oscar Wilde.

"Well, Pard, this is interesting."

She didn't look up. "What?"

"Says here that there have been two county sheriffs killed in the last month. Sheriff Miles Bradford of Clay County and Sheriff Sheriff Brad Jamison. Both shot from ambush...no leads."

Loraine finally looked up. "Oh, my, see what you mean. That is interesting...Think there's any connection?"

He glanced over at her. "Now what do you think, Pard?...Both the high sheriffs of their county...both shot from ambush by a high powered rifle, no clues, no suspects...Don't believe in coincidence, you? May have a serial killer here."

"You know I don't. So, what are you saying?"

"Saying we need to put our detective skills to use while we're here and check it out...before they work their way down to Jack County and Grandpa Flynn."

"Better not let him hear you call him that...or call your great grandmother, Fiona, Grannie...if you know what's good for you."

"Yeah, I know." He grinned. "Fiona'd peel my head like an onion...So, what do you think?"

"Think we should go check it out. I'm getting bored since we got back from the Kiamichis and helping Bass and them take care of that Teddy Roosevelt thing."

He grinned. "Thought you'd never bring it up."

§§

I hope you enjoyed BONE and the preview of the next novel in the series...BONE'S LAW. It's always appreciated if you liked the read to leave a favorable review on Amazon and Good Reads. Thank you,
Ken Farmer

Drop me a note any time. My email is:
pagact@yahoo.com

My Facebook page is:
www.facebook.com/KenFarmerAuthor

My author page on Amazon is:
www.amazon.com/default/e/B0057OT3YI

TIMBER CREEK PRESS

BLACKSTAR BAY by T.C. Miller
BLACKSTAR MOUNTAIN by T.C. Miller

HISTORICAL FICTION WESTERN
THE NATIONS by Ken Farmer and Buck Stienke
HAUNTED FALLS by Ken Farmer and Buck Stienke
HELL HOLE by Ken Farmer
ACROSS the RED by Ken Farmer and Buck Stienke
BASS and the LADY by Ken Farmer and Buck Stienke
DEVIL'S CANYON by Buck Stienke
LADY LAW by Ken Farmer
BLUE WATER WOMAN by Ken Farmer
FLYNN by Ken Farmer
AURALI RED by Ken Farmer
COLDIRON by Ken Farmer
STEELDUST by Ken Farmer
BONE by Ken Farmer

SY/FY
LEGEND of AURORA by Ken Farmer & Buck Stienke
AURORA: INVASION (Book #6 in the BEF) by Ken Farmer & Buck Stienke

HISTORICAL FICTION ROMANCE
THE TEMPLAR TRILOGY
MYSTERIOUS TEMPLAR by Adriana Girolami
THE CRIMSON AMULET by Adriana Girolami
TEMPLAR'S REDEMPTION by Adriana Girolami

Coming Soon

HISTORICAL FICTION WESTERN
NO TIME to DIE by Buck Stienke (sequel to
Devil's Canyon by Buck Stienke
BONE'S LAW by Ken Farmer

HISTORICAL FICTION ROMANCE
DAUGHTER of HADES by Adriana Girolami
ZAMINDAR and the LADY by Adriana Girolami
MILITARY ACTION/TECHNO
BLACKSTAR RANCH by T.C. Miller

SY/FY
ANTAREAN DILEMMA by T.C. Miller

Thanks for reading *BONE*. If you enjoyed it, I would really appreciate a review on Amazon. My Author Page is:

www.amazon.com/Ken-Farmer/e/B0057OT3YI

Email - pagact@yahoo.com

Personally autographed books available at my web site:

Web page: www.KenFarmer-Author.net

TIMBER CREEK PRESS